Amish Christmas

Blessing

Samantha Bayarr

Amish Christmas Blessing: Three Novellas

A NOTE FROM THE AUTHOR

While this story is set against the real backdrop of an Amish community, the characters and the town are fictional. There is no intended resemblance between the characters and community in this story and any real members of the Amish or communities. As with any work of fiction, I've taken license in some areas of research as a means of creating the necessary circumstances for my characters and the community in which they live. My research and experience with the Amish are quite knowledgeable; however, it would be impossible to be entirely accurate in details and description since every community differs, and I have not lived near enough to an Amish community for several years to know pertinent and current details. Therefore, any inaccuracies in the Amish lifestyle and their community portrayed in this book are due to fictional license as the author.

Table of Contents

Two women presented a baby to the king, each claiming to be his mother.

The king said, "Bring me a sword."

A sword was brought to the king.

He then gave an order.

"Cut the child in two and give half to one woman and half to the other."

Then the woman who was really the mother of the child, and who loved him very much, cried out.

"Oh no, my Lord, give her the child. Please do not kill him."

But the other woman said, "Neither I, nor you shall have him. Cut him in two!"

Then the king gave his ruling.

"Do not kill him, but give him to the woman who wants him to live, for she is his mother!"

1 Kings 3: 24-27

PART ONE AMISH CHRISTMAS

CHAPTER 1

"Quiet, Jonas," Zach hollered. "Do you hear that?"

"I don't hear nothing except that cow bawling because you ain't milkin' her fast enough," Jonas complained.

"You're both going to hear nothing but dad tanning your backside if you don't get them chores done," Jacob warned.

Zach fidgeted on the milking stool. "I don't like milking cows. I'm still too young."

Jacob looked over his shoulder at his youngest brother who was almost ten years old and too full of pride to keep *mamm* and *daed* from embarrassment in front of the bishop.

"If you're old enough to walk, you're old enough to milk that cow. Now get to work or there won't be any milk on the table for the morning meal and that won't make *mamm* very happy."

"But I know I heard something and it wasn't the cow," Zach complained.

What did it sound like?" Jonas asked.

"It sounded like a baby crying," Zach answered.

"All you hear is the wind whistling and the snow blowing around," Jacob said. "But you're going to be the one crying if you don't get them chores done."

Zach scowled. "You think you've got an answer for everything, don't you?"

"And you have a way of trying to get out of doing your chores every day."

Zach looked up at his older brother who was rubbing down the horses.

"But it's Christmas. Why do we have to do chores on Christmas?"

"The cows still need to be milked and the animals need to be cleaned up after and fed, just like you do!" Jacob said with a scowl.

Zach folded his arms across his chest and pouted out his lower lip.

"If you weren't the baby of the family you wouldn't get away with so much," Jacob complained.

"One of us has to be the baby," Zach said in his defense. "Since *mamm* can't have any more babies, she'd be sad without me."

"Just because *mamm* can't have any more babies doesn't mean she needs you to act like one. She needs you to pull your weight around here just like the rest of us," Jacob scolded.

Elijah walked over from mucking the stalls and nudged his younger brother off the milking stool.

Landing in the soft hay on the floor of the barn, Zach kicked at his brother vengefully.

"Why did you do that?" Zach cried.

"Because all you do is complain," Elijah said with a scowl.

"If he hadn't done it, I would have, and I'm sure that goes for the rest of your *bruders,*" Levi hollered, looking around at the other Fisher boys in the barn as they all nodded one-by-one in agreement. "If you want to be the baby so much then go be a girl, because that's what *mamm* wants. While you're at it, you can go fetch the eggs out of the henhouse because that's girl's work."

"We're all tired of hearing you run your mouth," Amos added. "*Mamm* will be expecting us, and we ain't even close to finishing the morning chores, so I agree, go fetch the eggs like a girl, because you ain't doing us no *gut* here."

Each of the six brothers rotated chores every morning before first light, and the day was wearing on, but they hadn't yet completed their chores due to Zach's lagging.

Zach stuck his tongue out at his five brothers as he opened the barn door and walked out into the swirling snow. He tucked his coat around him tightly and shoved his hands in his pockets as he walked toward the henhouse to fetch the eggs *like a girl*.

CHAPTER 2

Ellie Fisher turned from the chore of baking bread, wondering if her mind was playing tricks on her, but she could have sworn she'd heard a baby crying. She had not heard a buggy pull up to the house, and it was much too cold for anyone to travel by foot for a visit. Not to mention that today was first Christmas and the entire community would be at home with their own families.

Christmas was not something she was looking forward to this year, but rather, something she felt she had to *get through.* Certainly her recent news had put such sorrow in her heart that most days she'd had a difficult time finding joy in everyday living. It wasn't that Ellie was ungrateful for the six wonderful, strong sons that her husband, Jeremiah, had given her. It was that her life seemed to lack the one thing that she desired most, and that was to have a daughter of her own. Her desire as she grew older had put her in such a mood this year. Every year she'd hoped for a daughter, and this year would come and go without such a blessing, and that made her a little sad.

To have a daughter by her side was important to Amish women. It was how they handed down traditions and secrets of their lineage. Not to mention that she would have someone to work in the kitchen with her so she didn't have to do simple things like baking bread by herself. All the other women in the community had daughters to work side-by-side with their mother's, sewing and cooking and learning all the traditions that were handed down to them by their own mothers.

Ellie stared out the kitchen window mindlessly as she kneaded the bread dough. The wind whistled and howled, blowing in through the cracks of the windowsill, causing Ellie to shiver a bit. If not for the heat coming from the stove, Ellie would have wondered if she could freeze to death standing there.

She reached up and scraped at the ice on the inside of the window on the glass with her fingernail, taking note that her husband had long-since promised that he would replace that window. The stresses of life had somehow gotten in the way of such promises, and Ellie reflected on the many things that had fallen by the wayside during the stressful times the last couple of years had found them in.

Ellie had recently come to the realization that her monthly cycles had come to a halt, and the doctor at the clinic had told her that he didn't see any more *kinner* in her future. Those words had broken her heart more than he could know, but in her mind, she knew it to be true. Her body was too worn out to have any more children, and though her heart ached for a daughter, she leaned on God's strength to get her through the times like today when it bothered her the most.

Though she could not understand why it was that God had not answered her prayer and blessed her with a daughter, she had come to accept that it must be His will, and that it just was not going to be a part of her life. Still, she couldn’t help but hold onto that tiny bit of hope that God would fulfill her heart's desire and bless her just as she'd been praying for all those years.

Ellie split the dough and placed it into four baking pans, placing cheesecloth over each pan and then placed them near the stove so the dough would rise. As she wiped her hands, she heard once more a faint cry that seemed to be coming from the side door. *Perhaps one of the kittens got loose from the barn again*, she thought to herself. Zach was always leaving the barn door open. Ellie crossed the kitchen floor, intending to fetch the kitten and return it to the barn. But when she opened the door her heart did a somersault behind her rib cage.

At her feet, Ellie was shocked to see a baby wriggling and crying inside a small wicker basket. The infant had managed to pull the blankets free from its face. Though a small amount of snow had accumulated over the top of the blankets, Ellie could see the little face peeking through the opening. Bending down with shaky hands, Ellie reached for the basket and took it inside the warm kitchen with her. Shaking so much her teeth chattered, she set the basket on the table in the corner of the kitchen and carefully folded back the thick blankets to reveal an infant. Atop its head was a red and white striped hat. Instinct made her pick up the infant, holding it close to her warm body and comforting its cries. She tucked the baby's cool cheeks against the crook of her neck and walked over toward the warm stove, hoping that the heat would help to warm the newborn.

She bounced the infant slightly and cooed, enjoying the feel of the child in her arms. Was this real? Within minutes, the baby relaxed and quieted, falling asleep on her shoulder.

Still shaking, Ellie crossed to the basket, rifling through the blankets looking for any evidence of where the child belonged. Tucked in the folds of the blankets was a note. Ellie was almost too afraid to read it, but read it, she must. Without thinking, she ran to the door, swinging it open and looking for the whereabouts of the child's mother.

Taking notice of footprints in the snow that seemed to snake around behind the large oak tree in the side yard, and back toward the road, Ellie had to wonder how it was that someone had managed to leave the child without being noticed.

The infant shuddered in her arms, causing Ellie to shut the door quickly and go back toward the stove to keep the infant warm. Picking up the note once more, Ellie unfolded it, hoping that it contained an answer to her long-awaited prayer.

CHAPTER 3

Ellie opened the letter and read the lines she imagined had to have been painful for the mother to write.

Dear Amish family,

Please take my baby and raise it as your own. I am too young to take care of the baby and I don't have a husband. A friend told me I could drop off my baby off at the fire station or the hospital, but I didn't want my baby to be raised by strangers who might not love it. I know you already have a lot of children, but I hope you will have enough love in your heart for this baby too.

Thank you.

Ellie stared at the piece of paper and the very neat handwriting that gave no clues as to who the mother could be, other than *Englisch*. She held the sleeping infant close with trembling hands and a hopeful heart. Could this be a gift from God on this very day that his only son was also born?

Tears welled up in Ellie's eyes as she thought of the sacrifice this mother had made. Her tears of joy over this precious gift quickly turned to panic. Would Jeremiah agree to let her keep this baby? Surely, he would see what a miracle this child was, and on such a miraculous day as this. She couldn't have asked for a better gift.

But her husband was a practical man, and he would remind her that her childbearing years had long-since passed, and they were too old to raise the child.

Ellie lowered the baby and cradled it softly in her arms as she looked into the small, innocent face that already trusted her. Being the community midwife for more than fifteen years, she knew just by looking at the infant that it had been born only a few hours ago. She lifted the tiny shirt and red sweater taking note that the cord was still blue, and had been tied with twine. Pulling a piece of straw from the folds of the *Englisch* diaper, she suddenly wondered if the child had been born in a nearby barn. More than that, the note suggested the mother knew her family.

Ellie raised the letter in her trembling hand once more. The mother knew Ellie had many children. How could she know this detail, unless she knew them personally?

Her heart sank as she thought of the neighboring farms, realizing the only one close enough to travel by foot was the Yoder farm. Selma Yoder was the eldest in their community and had gone blind about a year ago. Her granddaughter, Anna, had come to live with her then, and had begun courting Ellie's oldest son, Jacob. The boy had been full of anger ever since Anna had broken it off between them without explanation. Jacob had refused to talk about what had happened between them.

New panic rose up in Ellie as she held the baby, suddenly wondering if it could be her very own grandchild. She studied the child's face noticing the dimples already formed in the tiny little cheeks, the same dimples her own Jacob wore every day. Love filled her instantly as the possibility of who this child could be sank into her heart. Surely if the child was her grandchild, Jeremiah would let them keep the baby.

Ellie's emotions ripped in several different directions. To have a grandchild for Christmas would be a wonderful gift. But reality soon sank in. The mother had not offered the child as a grandchild, but as a child to be raised by Ellie herself. Surely if the child belonged to her Jacob, the note would have said so.

No, the mother had stated she had no husband. If Anna had become pregnant by Jacob, surely there would have been a wedding a long time ago. She was certain Anna herself would have insisted on it. Besides, the baby was dressed in store-bought clothes—unless that was intentional to make her believe the baby was *Englisch.*

Ellie was suddenly startled when Jacob barreled into the kitchen toting the large pail from the morning milking.

"Whose baby is that?" He asked.

Ellie looked at him, unable to answer him just yet because she simply didn't know.

CHAPTER 4

Ellie's eyes darted back and forth between the infant in her arms and her grown son who stood before her, confusion clouding his expression.

"Hitch up the buggy for me," Ellie said to her son. "I have an errand to run."

"But *mamm,* it's Christmas."

"I know what day it is. Send Zach into the *haus* so he can go with me."

"Why does he always get to ditch his chores?"

"I'll be taking a Christmas pie over to the Yoder farm, and I'm going to need his help managing the infant."

"What should I tell *Daed* when he asks why you've left the *haus* on Christmas?"

"You tell him exactly where I went. He'll understand. But don't breathe a word about the *boppli.* I'd like to tell him myself."

Jacob did as his mother asked, and had the buggy waiting outside the kitchen door within a few minutes.

Soon enough, Zach was in the kitchen, underfoot, asking a million questions, but one really made her stand up and take notice.

"Does this mean I'm not your baby anymore?"

Ellie tucked her hand under her youngest son's chin, and bent down, placing a soft kiss on his forehead. She knew that all too soon he would not want so much to be her baby, and so for now, she would indulge his childish whims.

"*Nee*, it doesn't mean anything of the sort. But it does mean I need you to be a big *buwye* and go with me to the Yoder farm to deliver this Christmas pie."

"But what about that baby? Are we keeping it?"

"That is not up to us to decide, Zach. It is up to *Gott*."

"When is *Gott* gonna decide?"

"Soon, I pray," she answered.

Ellie placed the basket containing the sleeping infant in the back of the buggy and set the covered pie on Zach's lap for safe-keeping. Soon, they were traveling down the driveway toward their neighbor's farm.

"What do you suppose *Daed* will say about the baby?"

Admittedly, Ellie couldn't be certain of her husband's reaction, but Jeremiah was a good-natured man who had always been very fair with his family.

Unable to think past what she was about to encounter at the Yoder farm, Ellie dismissed her son's question as she pulled the buggy off the main stretch of the road, and into her neighbor's driveway.

The muffled clip-clip of the horse's hooves as they trampled down a path in the snow-covered drive put Ellie in a trance. She almost feared the reality that the child could belong to Anna. Had she made a mistake by bringing the child with her? What if Anna changed her mind about giving the child up when she saw it again? Should she risk such a thing? Surely if the child belonged to Anna, she could come back at any time and take the child from her. There would be nothing more than the note between them. Was that enough?

Ellie shook off her selfish thoughts as she pulled the buggy to a halt near the barn. Right away, Ellie noticed footprints in the snow near the barn door, as well as red splotches that looked like it could be blood. Fearing the worst, Ellie ordered her son to take the pie up to the house while she pulled the buggy into the barn.

"Why do I have to go up there by myself? She always stares at me and it makes me nervous."

"Zachary Fisher, that woman is blind! She's not staring at you, she's simply staring, that's all. Now do what I said, and tell her I'll be along just as soon as I pull the horse into the barn and out of this wind."

She could tell her son did not want to do as he was told, but Ellie could not allow her son to witness what mayhem she might be confronted with just beyond the door of the barn.

CHAPTER 5

Ellie waited for Zach to go into the house, and then opened the barn door wide enough to let the buggy through. She drove it into the holding area where the Widow Yoder's buggy sat. Her gaze fell upon small traces of blood on the wood planks that made up the floor of the barn. She retrieved the basket with the baby from the buggy and carried it up with her to see if Anna was alright. Knowing there was a small apartment in the loft of the barn, she wasn't sure if she should knock on the door or if she should just go in.

Deciding she should knock first, she did that and waited.

No answer.

Thinking she heard a groan, Ellie let herself into the apartment, worried that Anna could be in danger. She opened the door slowly, calling out for Anna. When she didn't find her in the main room of the apartment, Ellie walked toward the open bedroom door, calling out the girl's name again. As she approached the bed, where Anna lay groaning, Ellie knew immediately she was in danger. Taking into consideration the streaks of blood she saw on the sheets, Ellie tried to jiggle the girl's shoulder, hoping she would wake enough to know she was there.

"Anna, it's Ellie Fisher. I think I need to examine you to make sure everything is okay."

Being the midwife, she wasted no time in taking matters into her own hands for the sake of Anna's life. Taking note the girl had shed her jacket before crawling into the bed, Ellie could see that Anna had not changed out of her nightgown. Lifting the sheet, Ellie took a look to be sure she wasn't bleeding out.

Upon closer examination she could see the cord still dangling from Anna's body, the end tied with a piece of twine that matched the one attached to the infant. The young woman had not yet expelled the placenta and could be in danger of infection if it wasn't delivered. Utilizing the only natural means that she knew, she picked up the baby from the basket and set her to Anna's breast, knowing that it would bring on strong contractions that would help to expel the placenta. Within minutes, contractions began to expel the placenta. Relief washed over Ellie, and she was able to deliver the intact organ. Next, she knew it was important to stop the bleeding, so she began to knead Anna's lower abdomen like bread dough in order to clamp down her uterus.

Within minutes the bleeding slowed, and Ellie retrieved some fresh towels in the bathroom to put under the girl. Knowing she couldn't just leave her there alone, Ellie pulled the baby from her breast and tucked the child back into the basket. Then, she assisted Anna in sitting and helped her into her jacket. She tried assisting the sleepy young woman to her feet, but not before she noticed the box of sleeping pills at the bedside table.

Ellie laid her back down on the bed and opened the box, counting the remaining pills noting that only two were missing. Relieved that the girl had not taken more than the normal dose, Ellie assumed she'd taken them simply so she could rest.

"Anna, I need you to walk down the stairs and get into my buggy I'm going to take you home with me. Do you think you can walk with me?"

Anna groaned, but nodded her head, agreeing to go with Ellie.

She made quick work of getting Anna into the buggy, and then went back into the apartment to get the baby. Before pulling the buggy from the shelter of the barn, Ellie went up to the house to retrieve her son from the company of the Widow Yoder.

Ellie apologized that she couldn't stay, and wished the widow a Merry Christmas, excusing herself from the woman's company. It was obvious the older woman didn't know about Anna's condition, and Ellie didn't want to worry her unnecessarily. Not to mention, it simply was not her place to tell the woman of her granddaughter's business. That was between her and Anna.

Once in the buggy, Zach didn't miss the opportunity to complain.

"Why didn't you stay there and visit? Did you bring me here to punish me for not doing my chores?" Zach asked.

"Visiting a neighbor is not punishment, Zach."

Turning at the groan coming from the back of the buggy, Zach looked at his mother curiously.

"What is she doing back there? And what's wrong with her?"

"Mind your own business for now, Zach."

His mother reprimanded him, knowing she wasn't even certain how she was going to go about giving an explanation to her husband or to the son who used to date Anna.

Ellie pulled the buggy up to the barn and opened the door, sending Zach inside to retrieve his two older brothers to help her get Anna into the house. She knew her husband would still be working on the special *project* he'd been working on for the past few weeks, so he would be too preoccupied to know what was going on at the moment. It wasn't that she was trying to do anything behind her husband's back, for she knew he would be agreeable to helping a neighbor in need. He was an easy-going man who believed in helping other people in any way he could. She knew the visitor would not be a problem, but she wasn't sure about how to approach the letter from Anna, which gave them permission to raise the child.

Knowing Anna's current emotional state, Ellie would not address the letter with her husband until she'd had a chance to discuss it with the young woman. For everyone's peace of mind, she would make certain that it was Anna's final wish for them to raise her child before making the decision to discuss it with Jeremiah.

Jacob entered the kitchen just as his mother was setting down the basket with the baby on the table.

"What's wrong, *mamm*?" Jacob asked.

"I brought Anna Yoder back with me, and she's going to have to stay for a while until she recovers from the *birth*," his mother answered.

Jacob's face drained of all color as he looked at his mother for an answer he wasn't going to get.

"That child is hers?" Jacob stammered.

Realizing her son had no idea Anna was pregnant, Ellie knew that now was not the time to ask if the child was his.

"It is not for us to judge, Jacob, but we are able to take care of her in her time of need, and that is what we will do." His mother said sternly.

"No wonder she broke up with me," Jacob mumbled.

"There will be plenty of time to discuss this later," his mother reprimanded. "For now, I need you and your brother to get her out of the buggy before she freezes to death and get her up the stairs so she can rest."

"Where do you think we are going to put her, *mamm*?" Jacob asked.

"She's going to have to sleep in your room," his mother answered. "You can stay in the *dawdi haus* from here on out, Jacob."

Ellie thought she heard her son grumble under his breath as he went out to the buggy to help carry the young woman into the house, but she let it slide, knowing the seriousness of the situation and how much it must hurt Jacob to find out that Anna had a child without his knowledge.

She understood the heartbreak her son was suddenly experiencing, and she didn't blame him in the least, but she had to make him understand that now was not the time to let that out. Even she would keep the letter to herself for now, knowing that the contents would likely hurt her son. Her own wants and needs could wait.

If only for today alone, she had a new baby to care for, and a young woman to tend to, and that was all she could focus on for the moment.

CHAPTER 6

Once Anna was settled in Jacob's room, Ellie knew that she needed to take the crying infant to her once more for a feeding. She knew the likelihood of Anna giving up the child after bonding occurred was little to none, but the child needed to be fed and Ellie would put her own feelings aside for the sake of the child. It was no longer a matter of Anna giving up her child and Ellie accepting the child, it was now a matter of survival for both of them. Ellie knew that nursing the baby would help to keep Anna's bleeding to a minimum and help her recover sooner, and the baby needed the breast milk since it was so little, and it was the best form of nourishment.

Ellie entered the room quietly, infant cradled in her arms lovingly. She was already becoming attached to the infant, but she steeled her emotions against the thought of it, knowing it was best for the child and for Anna.

She put a soft hand to her shoulder, "I need you to wake up a little bit Anna," Ellie said. "You need to feed the *boppli*."

Anna's eyes sprang open unexpectedly and stared at her surroundings, confusion filling her expression. "Where am I?"

"I brought you home with me so I could take care of you while you recover from the birth."

Ellie gently bounced the cranky infant in her arms as she tried to reason with Anna. "Right now, this wee one needs to be fed, and I need your help with that."

Anna stiffened her lip and turned her head defiantly. "Take her away, she's yours. I gave her to you; please leave me alone." Anna sobbed.

The sudden realization that the infant Ellie was holding was indeed a little girl, hit her like an ice storm. A little girl of her own was what she had prayed for. Was it possible this was *Gott's* answer to her prayer?

"*She*," Ellie said, biting back tears and nearly choking on the word. "Needs to be fed, as she cannot be more than 6 pounds, and I need you to think of her right now instead of yourself."

Ellie wanted so much to be selfish right now as well, but she knew the child needed to be fed, and breast milk was the best thing for her, given her size.

"We could both be selfish right now," Ellie said sternly. "But right now this *boppli* needs to be fed and you and I need to work together to ensure her survival."

"Why didn't you just leave me there to die a sinner's death? That is what I deserve," Anna sobbed.

Tears welled up in Ellie's eyes as she sat down on the bed beside Anna. Laying the infant down beside her, Ellie leaned down and pulled Anna into her arms and held her while she sobbed.

"We are all sinners, Anna," Ellie said softly. "And if we all deserved to die for our sins, there wouldn't be a single person living on this earth. The best way you can make up for the sin is to make it right by taking care of what God blessed you with."

Anna pulled away from Ellie and looked at her as she wiped her eyes. "Is it really that easy?" She asked. "All I have to do is take care of the baby, and God will forgive me?"

"An act of kindness alone will not bring forgiveness," Ellie corrected. "But *Gott* knows what's in your heart, and that is where you will find forgiveness."

"I will feed her so she will survive," Anna said with a sniffle. "But I gave her to you to raise because that is the right thing to do. She needs a proper home, and I just can't give that to her."

"We don't have to talk about that right now while you're emotional. Let's sleep on it and give it another day." Ellie suggested. "I will do whatever is in *Gott's* will for this child, and that is not for us to decide."

Anna nodded as she allowed Ellie to place the infant at her breast. Ellie rose from the bed, excusing herself momentarily as she swallowed the lump that formed in her throat. The little girl was what she'd always dreamed of. It was what she'd prayed for, but she knew now was not the time to give in to those wants.

"There will be silence at the table this evening as we reflect on the blessings this day has brought our *familye,*" Jeremiah ordered his sons. "Today is Christmas, and we will reflect on the miracle of birth: both the birth of our Lord, and the birth that we have been blessed to share with Anna today. And it will be done without judgment."

Each of his sons nodded quietly, and then returned to their meal.

Ellie had not had much of an opportunity to explain the situation to her husband, but what she did explain was enough for him to understand that there was a new family in need, and they would care for the needs of that family no matter what the circumstances. There would be plenty of time later to find out the where and why, but for now, that would remain Anna's business until she was ready to talk about it or share it with them. As a family, they would help her and the child because that was what the season was all about.

Everyone turned when they heard a creak on the back steps to the kitchen. Though Ellie tried to jump up right away to assist Anna, it was not quick enough to prevent the scowl from spoiling Jacob's expression.

"I thought this was a day for family," Jacob complained as he threw down his napkin. "If she's coming down to have Christmas dinner with us, I'm leaving."

"Jacob," his father scolded. "You will sit and finish your meal with the rest of the family, and if our guest wants to join us, you will stay."

Anna turned on the stairwell, apologizing for disrupting their meal, as she tried to make her way back upstairs quickly. Ellie excused herself with a nod to her husband, and he nodded his consent for her to help. Ellie caught up with Anna in the stairwell, looping her arm on the young woman's, and assisted her up the stairs. She tucked her back in the bed, offering to bring up a tray of food if she was hungry, but Anna would not say a word. She wouldn't even look her in the eye.

"I'm sorry," Anna cried. "My presence here seems to be upsetting your son. I should leave."

"As long as I have something to say about it, you do not have to leave. You will stay as long as it takes to recover, and my son will be reprimanded for his behavior."

"Don't discipline Jacob on my account. If I didn't fear for my for my health I would leave immediately."

"You will do no such thing," Ellie said kindly. "You are a guest in our home, and in need of help. We will help you as long as you need us."

"I don't deserve help from anyone," Anna cried. "I don't deserve anything from anyone."

"That is not true, Anna. Only *Gott* knows what you do or don't deserve, and I can tell you right now you do deserve to be cared for. No matter what you've done."

"It doesn't matter," she cried. "I will be leaving as soon as I am able to."

Ellie did not want Anna to leave under these circumstances, even though she was eager for a decision to be made regarding the infant.

Ellie tried to comfort Anna, but she turned her face toward the wall, crying quietly and ignoring any comfort. Ellie let herself out of the room and went down to be with her family. Ellie looked at her son, Jacob. Though she felt sorry for him, she was disappointed in the way he'd acted out.

"You will apologize to Anna," she reprimanded her son.

"Apologize to her?"

"You will not raise your tone with your *mamm*," his father scolded.

"*Daed*, why should I apologize to her? She got herself pregnant when I wanted to marry her."

Jeremiah furrowed his brow as he scanned the faces of his sons who sat at the table with eager faces, hoping to find out their brother's business.

"I said there will be silence at this meal, and there will be silence, Jacob. We will speak of this at the end of the meal, but not before then."

The room fell silent again except for the clanging of utensils on the plates and the occasional clearing of someone's throat. It was too quiet, quiet enough to give Ellie too much time to think, and she did not want to think too much at the moment.

CHAPTER 7

Though Ellie wanted to stay and hear what Jacob had to say about marrying Anna, she knew that it was a talk better discussed with his father than with her. Besides, she had to take care of the baby. After the feeding time with Anna, Ellie tried to encourage Anna to bond with the baby since she hadn't yet shown any interest, but all she would do was turn her face away from the child. Part of Ellie was content knowing that Anna had no interest in the child and was still willing to allow her to raise her, but the other part of her worried Anna was basing her decision on her inability to care for the child. Ellie wanted to offer her assistance, but she knew that now was not the time, as Anna was far too emotional to hear anything she would have to say about the child. She would have to rely on God to show them both the truth and the way so that His will would be done and not their own.

Ellie took the baby downstairs to the kitchen and filled the sink with warm water, and then gathered some clean towels from the bathroom, going about the task of readying the baby for her bath. She knew that bathing her near the kitchen stove would keep the baby from getting too cold. She quickly pulled a spool of surgical thread and a pair of shears from her birthing bag so she could tie the cord closer to the baby's abdomen.

Ellie felt suddenly grateful that she had the things the local clinic supplied her with that allowed her to take care of the women in her community.

As she undressed the squirming baby for her first bath, she reflected on each time she'd given her own children their first bath. First baths were special, as were all *firsts* with her babies. But this wee one was not yet hers, and she dared not hope that it be true, lest her heart would break if it didn't come to pass. Already, it would be difficult to hand the infant over to Anna, should the young woman decide she wanted to raise her after all. Either way, it was going to be a tough decision for one of them to have to give up the child.

Being reminded Anna had left such a large length of cord hanging from the baby, Ellie went about the task of tying and cutting the cord before undressing the baby fully. Once accomplished, she wrapped the baby in a towel and held her head over the warm water as she splashed it over her to wash her soft little head. After washing her wisps of sandy hair, she quickly dried her and went about cleaning the rest of her, keeping her on the counter near the warm stove. Ellie made fast work of the bath since the baby's lips chattered and she cried so heartily. Having not had time to wash the clothing Jeremiah had fetched from the attic, Ellie was grateful there was an extra set of clothing and paper diapers in the bottom of the basket Anna had put her daughter in.

Though it was not washday, Ellie would have to wash the tiny items of clothing in order for the baby to have something clean to wear the following day. She would hang them across the fireplace hearth to dry them quickly and to keep them warm for the tiny infant.

Once she had the baby washed and dried, she put a clean diaper and clothes on her, intending to take her back to Anna for another feeding before the household retired for the night. Jeremiah had brought in the boy's cradle from the barn and placed it next the Ellie's side of the bed so she could get up and take her in to Anna for her feedings during the night. Ellie wished that there was another way, but for now she knew the feedings would help the child thrive.

Thankfully, Anna was sleepy, and did not make any conversation when Ellie took the baby to her for her feeding, nor did she resist in any way. Ellie did not have the energy to debate with the girl any more regarding the importance of nursing the child.

At the conclusion of the feeding, Ellie took her downstairs to rock her to sleep and to burp her. Jeremiah pulled the rocking chair closer to the fireplace and stoked the fire. Then he kissed his wife and smiled, telling her he would see her in a few minutes upstairs.

Ellie sat in the rocker and held the baby girl in her arms, nuzzling her and kissing her soft, pink cheeks. So this was what it felt like to have a little girl. She rocked the infant, singing her favorite

Ausbund hymns, thinking to herself how much she already loved the little girl, and how hard it would be if *she* was the one that had to give her up when all was said and done.

CHAPTER 8

By the time Ellie returned to her room with the baby, her husband was already fast asleep. He'd been working very hard for the past couple of weeks on a gift for her for Christmas, but as she held the baby in her arms, she couldn't think of a better gift than the little girl. She wasn't sure anything could compare to the gift of the child she held so lovingly in her arms, the child she was afraid to let go of.

Reluctantly, Ellie kissed the baby once more and placed her in the cradle, tucking her neatly into the folds of the quilt. Then, as she climbed into bed, she was grateful for her husband and for his love and his patience with her during all the years that she'd hoped for a daughter. He'd been patient and understanding through every mood swing she'd experienced over the years when each month went by with no baby. Then again when she got the devastating news that she was no longer able to have children. She'd pushed it aside, trying not to think too much about it, but yet it was always in the back of her mind, and each month that went by hardened her heart even more.

Ellie rolled over, dangling her hand inside the cradle beside the bed, placing her finger into the wee one's hand. Little fingers gripped hers just as she gripped Ellie's heart. Ellie closed her eyes, blinking against the tears that formed there.

"Please *Gott,* bless me with the strength to do your will where this child is concerned. Bless me with the wisdom to know what is best for this little girl, and if what's best is to be with her mother and not me, then let your will be done."

Sometime later, Ellie woke up as the baby began to stir. Her eyes drifted to the window as she watched snowflakes flutter against the glass. They shimmered in the moonlight, floating like feathers in the hen house. The baby woke up, her little face turned toward Ellie, bright eyes looking up at her.

Ellie couldn't help but wonder what the future held for this child. She knew how she would care for the baby. She imagined days like the ones she'd had with her sons. She imagined sewing little dresses and making little *kapps*, and then teaching the little girl how to sew them herself. She imagined the two of them gathering eggs in the hen house and baking cookies in the kitchen, making a mess of the flour.

As she lifted the infant from the cradle and held her close, Ellie realized that all those things were not for her to do with this child, but for her mother. She was not this child's mother, but if it be God's will, she would be.

Ellie crept down the hall toward her son's room where Anna was sleeping and recovering. She knocked lightly on the door before entering, but Anna was already awake. Ellie was glad she did not have to force the feeding on Anna, but at the same time, Anna seemed ready for it and even willing.

Ellie walked over to the window watching the snow fall. Her mind drifted along with each snowflake that fell as she listened to Anna coo to her baby. Already Ellie mourned the loss of the child in her arms as she listened to Anna bond with the child in the darkness of the room.

Before long, Ellie could hear the child becoming restless.

"Take her away now," Anna said abruptly.

She turned away from the baby and closed her eyes while Ellie lifted the child from her side. She left the room swiftly without a word to Anna. She shifted the baby in her arms gently to release a burp from her, then placed her back into the cradle quickly to avoid having her waking up. Then she crawled in next to her husband, weeping quietly. Jeremiah gently pulled her toward him and kissed the back of her neck, shushing her lovingly.

"I know this must be difficult for you, taking care of that little girl when you can't have your own." Her husband said quietly.

"But Anna gave her to me," Ellie said.

"What do you mean she gave her to you?"

"She left her on our doorstep in a basket with a note giving me permission to raise her as my own. I put the pieces of the puzzle together and figured out the child must belong to Anna. That is why I went to her and brought her back here with me—because she was in distress."

"I wish you would've told me this sooner," Jeremiah whispered. "Perhaps I could've been more help if I'd known."

"There isn't anything any of us can do right now except sleep on it."

"And pray," Jeremiah said. "But we will have our answer in time. In the meantime we should pray for grace and peace for Anna."

Ellie wiped her eyes, knowing her husband was right. Grace and peace was exactly what they needed.

CHAPTER 9

Ellie woke up again when the baby stirred. She rose to change her, realizing there were only a few diapers left in the pack of disposables that Anna had packed into the bottom of the laundry basket she'd brought the child in.

She'd forgotten how much work an infant was, with night feedings, washing diapers and clothes constantly. But how would she feed the child once Anna was gone? The young woman had left a can of formula and a bottle in the basket, but Ellie had never bottle-fed her babies, and wasn't certain she knew how to do such a thing. She had been raised with the idea that breast milk was best for the child, and she'd never considered the alternative. How would she be able to raise this child differently?

She simply couldn't. There were no two ways about it. This child had already become dependent on her natural mother, and it would be cruel to break her from that. Not to mention the amount of work it would be for Ellie to bottle-feed a baby. And at her age, it suddenly dawned on her why it was God had not blessed her with the baby she had wanted so much.

She was just too old and worn out.

At fifty years old, God knew what she needed, even if she didn't. She would certainly care for the child if that was God's will, but she would have to pray for the physical and emotional strength to do it. This was only her second time up with the child, and only the first night, and she was already exhausted.

But what if this was a test from God?

She was certainly willing enough to raise the child if it was His will, but she was beginning to wonder if God didn't have something else in mind for her and the child.

Ellie let herself into the room where Anna was resting, but realized she was awake again. It was obvious that her body was waking her, letting her know it was feeding time. It was an instinct Ellie knew all too well. She handed the baby to Anna, and this time, she was able to place the baby at her breast without any help. Ellie could tell she was getting used to it.

"Have you thought about what you're going to name this wee one?" Ellie asked.

"I already told you I gave her to you," Anna answered sharply. "You name her."

"If it be up to me, I would name her Grace because it means blessing, and that's what this child is, a blessing."

Anna didn't say a word to her about it, and that bothered Ellie just a little bit. It would seem that Anna was still of the mindset of giving up the baby, but she wondered if time might cause her to change her mind. She supposed time was the only thing that would matter in the situation, something they didn't have much of. Within a couple of days Anna would be well enough to leave Ellie's home, and if she decided to keep the baby, Grace would be leaving too. Though Ellie wasn't sure if she was ready for that, she knew she had better prepare her heart for such a thing, just in case.

Ellie shot up in bed when the rooster crowed the second time, her heart racing out of control. Had she overslept? Leaning over the side of the bed, her sleepy gaze met with an empty cradle. She turned to her husband, but he was gone too. Tears welled up in her eyes, clogging her throat, as she threw on her robe and stuffed her cold feet into her slippers. She ran down the hall toward Anna's room, panic driving her. Not bothering to knock, Ellie threw open the door, startling Anna, who put a finger to her lips, shushing Ellie. There beside her, was Grace, sleeping soundly.

"I just got her to sleep," Anna whispered. "Please don't wake her up. I don't want to hear her cry anymore."

Ellie nodded as she picked up the sleeping baby.

"I'm so glad you finally came in here. I didn't know if Zach was going to come back for her or not," Anna complained.

Relief washed over Ellie as she held Grace close to her, realizing her husband must have brought the baby downstairs so she could get some sleep. She was certain Jeremiah had met with some grumbling when he'd asked their youngest son to bring the baby to Anna for feeding, but Ellie would have asked Jacob to do it instead, even though he'd have probably been the most resistant.

Once she was out of the room with Grace, Ellie breathed easier, but it bothered her how much fear had come over her when she'd thought Anna had left and had taken Grace with her. She had already grown so attached to the baby, but it was sadly obvious that Anna had not. Was it fear that kept her from bonding with her child, or was it something deeper that Ellie did not understand?

In the kitchen, Ellie found the infant seat that her sons used to sit in when they were babies. It was a tiny little cradle-like infant seat that her husband had made for them, and it was ideal for setting them on the counter while she worked. Placing Grace in the seat and wrapping her in the little tiny quilt, Ellie set to work making breakfast for her brood.

Before long, the kitchen was filled with the smells of sizzling bacon, fresh brewing coffee and cinnamon bread; the very things that brought her to life every morning. This was what her life was; it was taking care of the children that God had blessed her and Jeremiah with. Suddenly, she looked into Grace's little face, and she knew what she had to do. She had to do everything in her power to help Anna be at ease with her child so she could raise her. As much as she wanted little Grace to be her own, Ellie knew she needed to stifle her own selfish wants and do what was best for Grace and help Anna raise her. She could feel it in her spirit.

CHAPTER 10

Anna cried quietly as she lay in Jacob's bed, wondering how life might have been if she'd done right by him. She hadn't even done right by herself either, but least of all, she had ruined things for her daughter. It no longer mattered. Grace was now Ellie's child. Anna could not let her own selfish desires to raise little Grace to get in the way of having good judgment where her well-being was concerned. It would not be easy to leave this place, and it would not be easy to leave her child behind a second time, but she would do what was best for Grace no matter how much it broke her heart to do it.

A heavy knock startled her. Surely that was not Ellie's knock, and it wasn't possible that it was feeding time for the baby this soon. She wiped her eyes and lay there quietly, hoping that whoever it was would think she was asleep and go away.

Anna felt panic run through her veins like ice when the door opened and a familiar baritone spoke softly to her.

"Anna, *mei mudder* thought you would be hungry this morning, so she sent me with a tray of food for you."

He tiptoed into the room and set the tray on the bedside table while Anna kept her back to him. She knew she should say something to him, but what? What was there to say after all was said and done? Would mere words of apology mean anything to him? Still, it was now or never, and she had to make things right. It was the only way she could move forward.

"I'm sorry, Jacob," Anna whispered.

It was all she could say even though she knew it would never be enough. Jacob stopped and turned around to look at Anna.

Instead, he stared out the window at the snow. "I'm sorry I gave you an ultimatum that night. Obviously, I've changed my mind since then. I was full of big ideas then, and I thought that if I could live like an *Englischer* things would be different."

"As you can see, living like the *Englisch* did me no good," Anna said, sniffling. "I've made a big mistake and messed up too many lives because I thought I had all the answers. I thought things would be so much better out there away from our families, and they are not."

Jacob walked over to the window and stared out at the thick snow. "You don't owe me any explanation, Anna. This is not my business."

"I'm sorry my mistakes have hurt you. But this is what happens when a naïve Amish girl thinks that she can keep up with rowdy *Englisch* girls who tell her drinking a beer will take all her troubles away. All that beer did was put me in harm's way and now I have Grace because of it."

Jacob turned and looked at Anna soulfully.

"I'm so sorry you had to experience such a thing. I wish I could have spared you the hurt."

Anna began to weep. "Now you see why I could not marry you when you asked me. I could not present myself to you as a soiled bride."

"I would've married you anyway," Jacob whispered.

Anna began to cry even more. "The only thing that has saved me in all of this is the fact that my grandmother is blind and could not see that I was growing with child. I thought for certain that if I gave up the baby to your mother it would be the best thing for her. I still do."

"I realize that if the Bishop finds out about this you will surely be shunned, but you don't have to worry about *mei familye* telling him. I'm sorry this has happened to you and to Grace, but I just don't know how to help you other than keeping your confidence. I wish I could do more."

"Your *mamm* has already done so much for me by agreeing to raise Grace as her own. She will have a *gut familye* with all of you."

Jacob left the room feeling confused and completely helpless, but wondering if there wasn't a way to give Grace a better family than what Anna proposed.

CHAPTER 11

Ellie arranged a dessert tray and brought it into the sitting room for her family. Since they had not taken the time to exchange gifts the previous day because of all the excitement, they chose to do so at this time. It had been a long two days, and she was nothing short of exhausted.

Ellie tucked Grace over her shoulder as she sat down next to her youngest son.

"*Mamm* got a gift from Anna," Zach complained. "Do I get two gifts?"

Jeremiah scowled at his son. "You must not give in to greed, Zach," He reprimanded.

Each of Ellie's sons enjoyed homemade gifts from her ranging from the gloves and scarves, to a quilt Levi was desperately in need of. When it came time for Zach's gift, he was presented with a scooter his father had made. The ten-year-old quickly excused himself as he ran out the front door to ride his scooter along the wraparound porch in front of the house. When each of their children swiped several cookies from the tray and ran off, Jeremiah presented Ellie with her gift.

They didn't normally handle things this way, but this Christmas had changed them all because of Anna's and Grace's presence in their house. Ellie nearly cried when she saw the beautifully hand-carved nativity her husband had made her. Running her fingers along the manger and touching the top of the head of the baby Jesus, Ellie reflected on the baby in her own arms. God himself had sacrificed his only son, and Ellie knew she must do the same with Grace. She would sacrifice her own desires for what was best for little Grace.

It had upset her every time she'd taken the baby in for feeding with Anna when the young woman had pulled away from her child. It broke Ellie's heart to know that Grace would never be her child, but more than that, she hated seeing the hurt in Anna's eyes every time she brought the infant to her for feeding. The young woman simply refused to even look at the baby, much less, to let her guard down long enough to enjoy Grace. She thought she'd detected a little softness in her heart, but she'd stifled it too soon.

Ellie had talked things over with Jeremiah, and they had decided to offer the *dawdi haus* to Anna and Grace. Knowing the bishop would likely shun her for having a child out of wedlock, the Fishers decided they would have to treat her as an *Englisch* border. It wasn't the most ideal of circumstances for Anna and her child, but it would give them a good head start to a future.

It saddened Ellie that Anna would likely never be able to marry an Amish man, mostly because none would have her, but at least she would have Grace. And Ellie would help her raise her instead of raising her on her own. She hoped it would make a difference to the young woman and help convince her that the Fishers only wanted what was best for her and Grace. She hoped that this would be the most ideal situation for everyone involved.

Not only could she look after little Grace herself and enjoy time with her, Ellie would be on hand to teach her how to be a good mother. In exchange, Anna could help her in the kitchen and on laundry day, and that would be an advantage to Ellie. She didn't imagine it could be the same as having her own daughter, but Ellie would be content to have Anna's and Grace's company.

CHAPTER 12

At the evening meal Jacob surprised his parents by offering to take a tray to Anna once again. Ellie had not yet had the opportunity to speak to Anna about what she and Jeremiah talked about regarding her, but she planned to speak to her about it at the next feeding for Grace. She hoped that it would be received well by Anna, and that she would see the opportunity in this for her and Grace to be a family. It was a sacrifice that Ellie knew she had to make in order to accommodate for the best future for Grace.

"Don't upset the girl," Jeremiah warned his son. "Be respectful of her privacy, and don't upset her."

Jacob nodded as he walked up with the tray his mother had assembled for him. Once up the stairs, it felt foreign for Jacob to knock on his own bedroom door, but he did it out of respect for Anna. The last thing he wanted was for her to be upset. He wanted to make things right for her and for Grace, but he just wasn't sure how.

He didn't know if it was too soon to propose the idea he'd been tossing around in his mind because he didn't want to scare her off at a time when she was so emotional. He'd learned his lesson about giving the young woman an ultimatum, and he wouldn't repeat that mistake. He would simply make an offer to her, and if she refused, he would respect her decision and do his best to help her in any way he could, regardless of whether she rejected or accepted.

When Anna didn't answer his knock, he let himself in the room cautiously, feeling the need to sound a warning to her as he entered.

"Anna, it's me, Jacob. I'm bringing in a tray of food for you."

Anna faced the wall, but Jacob had a feeling she was awake.

"Are you awake Anna?"

Anna sniffled. "Just leave the tray. I'm not hungry."

"I know you're having a hard time with this, but you must keep up your strength in order to feed Grace."

"I gave her to your *mamm* to raise. I don't want to feed her anymore because it hurts too much. Your *mamm* can feed her with the bottle because I'll be leaving in the morning."

Jacob walked over to the window and put two fingers between the sheer curtains, separating them so he could watch the snow. "I'd like you to stay."

Anna sat up in the bed, wiping the tears from her eyes and sniffling.

"I can't stay here," she squealed. "I don't want to depend on your *familye*, and I don't want to get attached to Grace any more than I already am. I need to leave so your *mamm* can raise her has her own. I made a bad choice that brought her into this world. I won't make a bad decision where she's concerned again I've made my choice, and it's what's best for her."

"I think you're making a big mistake, Anna, and I'd like you to stay."

"I can't stay here and watch while another woman raises my baby. It's best if I leave. I won't be doing her or anyone else any good by staying here," Anna cried.

Jacob blew out a discouraging sigh. "I think I'm going about this all wrong. What I meant to say, is that I'd like to give Grace a last name."

Jacob crossed the room and sat on the edge the bed, pulling Anna into his arms as she wept.

"This isn't how it's supposed to be," Jacob said jokingly. "My proposal was not supposed to get this kind of reaction from you."

"I'm crying," Anna said, her words catching in her throat. "Because I can't marry you. That would not be fair to you or to Grace. Let your *mamm* raise her as her own. It would make them both happy. Besides, I wouldn't want you to marry me because you feel obligated, or because you feel sorry for me."

"I want to marry you, Anna, because I still love you. I've been angry because I've missed you so much. You think about it. Let me know your answer before you leave here."

Jacob pressed his lips against Anna's, placing a gentle, but brief kiss over her quivering lips. He would not push her for more, even though he wanted to lay claim over her mouth. Now was not the time after all she'd been through. Now was the time to prove to her that he respected her, unlike Grace's father had done. Jacob rose from the edge of the bed and left the room before she could reject him a second time.

CHAPTER 13

Ellie hung the last of the clean diapers on a wooden rack near the fireplace, hoping they would dry quickly. Little Grace was proving that she could go through diapers faster than Ellie's sons had. Now that she was bathed, Grace was ready for her last feeding for the night before Ellie would try to get some much-needed sleep.

Ellie knocked before entering the room where Anna rested. She had to admit she was a little nervous about her impending talk with Anna, but she knew deep down in her heart it was what was best for little Grace. She kissed the wee one on the top of her head before handing her down to Anna, though she didn't want to let her go.

Anna turned her back to the baby and faced the wall. "I told Jacob to let you know not to bring her to me anymore. Didn't he tell you?"

Jacob had not said a word to his mother about what Anna was saying now. How could she convince this young woman what she was about to offer her was what was best for her and Grace?

"Jacob did not tell me your wishes. But I have an offer that I hope you will consider. An offer that I pray will be best for everyone."

Anna just sat there with her back to her, so Ellie continued.

"I love Grace," Ellie said, choking back tears. "But after taking care of her the past two days, I have come to realize that I am just too old to raise her. She needs a young *mamm*. She needs you."

"She doesn't need me," Anna cried. "I've messed up her life simply by bringing her into this world."

Ellie put a hand on Anna's shoulder, hoping it would comfort her.

"That isn't true. The fact that you brought her here and wanted her to have a better life proves how much you love her. We both love her and we both think that the other should raise her, but only one of us can raise her and be her *mamm*. That person should be you since you are already her *mamm*."

"I can't be her *mamm*. I don't have a way to support her, and I don't have a husband, even though Jacob offered to marry me."

Ellie's heart did a somersault behind her ribcage. She had no idea her son would make such an offer. Was it possible that he still loved Anna as much she thought he did? As hard as it would be for Ellie, she knew she needed to convince Anna that accepting Jacob's offer was the right thing to do.

"Did you accept his proposal?"

"*Nee,*" she sobbed. "Jacob deserves better than me."

"Do you love Jacob?"

"*Jah,* I do," Anna sobbed. "But I don't deserve his love or his offer because of what I've done."

"I shouldn't pry this way, but did Jacob tell you he still loved you?"

"*Jah*, he did. But I don't deserve his love after what I've done."

Anna's shoulders shuddered as she wept heavily.

"Everyone makes mistakes Anna, but it's how you handle those mistakes and learn from them that's important. If my son loves you, and he made an offer of marriage, it wasn't an empty offer, and he surely believes you are worthy of his love. I also believe you are worthy of his love."

Anna wiped her eyes and looked at Ellie.

"You do?"

"I really do, Anna," Ellie confessed. "My husband and I were going to offer you the opportunity to move into the *dawdi haus* with Grace, but now you can be married to my son and you can live there together as a *familye.* You can raise your daughter."

Anna threw her arms around Ellie's neck and hugged her, thanking her repeatedly.

"I am happy that I am here to help you and Grace even if it's not to raise her as my own daughter."

"I know that could not have been an easy decision for you," Anna confessed. "Jacob told me how much you've always wanted a daughter of your own. That's why I left Grace here with you."

Ellie giggled happily. "With you married to Jacob I will have a daughter. You will be my daughter and Grace will be my granddaughter."

Ellie was truly happy with the outcome of her talk with Anna, the talk that she had dreaded for no reason at all.

Ellie kneaded the bread dough while Anna prepared the pans. The Widow Yoder, Anna's grandmother, cooed at little Grace as she sat on the table in the homemade chair that Jacob, her new father, had once sat in as an infant. Ellie's house was full and so was her heart. Not only had she been blessed with a daughter to work in the kitchen with her, she had been blessed with a granddaughter and even a new *mamm* for herself, since her own *mamm* had passed on a few years back, and the Widow Yoder was all-too happy to fill those shoes.

Yes, Ellie was truly happy, knowing that her unselfish act had brought her so much joy.

Zach suddenly burst into the kitchen, tracking snow and ice across the floor, as he ran to his *mamm's* side.

"Levi kicked me out of the barn again *mamm*," Zach complained. "He told me I had to fetch the eggs, saying I have to be your girl."

Ellie laughed at her son's dilemma. "As you can see, Zach, I have a kitchen full of girls, and I need you to be my son. You can fetch the eggs if you want to, but that doesn't make you a girl."

Zach looked up at his mother and smiled.

"Can I still be your baby?" He asked.

Ellie smiled as she hugged her son. "Zach, you will always be my baby."

PART TWO: AMISH GRACE

CHAPTER 14

Twenty-one years later...

Grace nudged one of the barn cats with her foot to keep it from dipping its little pink tongue into the pail of milk she'd set under her family's milking cow, Willow. Just a few more pulls on the udder and she would have a full pail, and she was not about to start over again because of a greedy kitten looking to spoil the batch by lapping in it.

"*Daed* says you shouldn't give into gluttony," she reprimanded the kitten as if it understood her. "But since he isn't my *daed* any more than he is yours, I suppose that keeps us from being bound by his teachings."

Grace thought about it for a minute.

"Perhaps the difference between right and wrong is still the same no matter who tells it to you."

Grace pushed the udder sideways and squirted a stream of milk toward the kitten as she delighted in his accuracy at lapping it up. The tuft of fur beneath his chin was milky-white and saturated, but he didn't let a single drop hit the barn floor.

She let out a sigh. "Be thankful you don't have to worry about who your *daed* is—or even who you are, for that matter."

Grace wished her parents had not told her the story of her birth, or about how she'd come to be in this world. She understood her *mamm's* fears as a young girl, and not knowing how she would provide for a baby without a husband. She had a lot of respect for her *daed* for loving her *mamm* enough to marry her, despite her mistake. But she wished they would have kept it to themselves. Especially now with her decision about marrying Seth Yoder weighing so heavily on her mind.

Today was the day she'd promised to give him her answer, and she could no more make up her mind about marrying him than she could make sense of her messed up thoughts about her family life. Never mind that she'd always wondered why she didn't quite seem to fit in with her family. She was a complete klutz in the kitchen, and she looked nothing like her siblings *or* her parents. She didn't even resemble her Grandma Ellie or Grandpa Jeremiah, or any of her *onkels,* and certainly not any of her many cousins. She was definitely the *black sheep* of the family, if ever there was one—or at least, the blonde-haired, blue-eyed sheep!

"If only I hadn't been nosing around in the attic where I didn't belong. Then I wouldn't have found that little red and white striped stocking cap, and they wouldn't have had to tell me the truth," Grace complained aloud.

The little black and white kitten rubbed against Grace's leg and purred. "Well, now you're just being greedy, and I'm in no mood to cater to you this morning, you spoiled little kitty."

She squirted one last stream of milk toward the animal, unable to resist his begging. Then, she raised from the milking stool and lifted the full pail, hoping she could slip it into the kitchen without her *mamm* stopping her for a chat.

She didn't want to talk.

She didn't want to think.

What she really wanted to do was escape from her problems and come back when she'd sorted it all out. But she couldn't do that.

Could she?

CHAPTER 15

Grace entered the kitchen with tip-toed silence, hoping she could make it back out to the hen house for the eggs without so much as a word from any of her family. Her younger siblings, Lilly, Becca, and Jonah were already finished with their chores and washing for breakfast.

Her *mamm* was pulling loaves of banana bread from the oven and gave her a look.

"I've been waiting on that milk, Grace. What's kept you?"

My brain hasn't been working right since you pulled my whole world out from under me yesterday, Grace thought.

She looked up at her *mamm* blankly as she headed for the back door.

"Never mind the eggs," her *mamm* scolded her. "Lilly got them."

Of course she did because Lilly does everything right!

Grace looked over at her younger sister who sneered at her. She was *mamm's* favorite. She could do everything that Grace could not, and the girl was always rubbing her nose in it. There had only been one thing Grace had been able to do right, and that was helping with Jonah. Since Jonah had come a little early, he was considerably small, and Grace was the only one who felt comfortable enough to hold him, and could therefore soothe him when he got colicky. But Lilly, sadly, had no interest when he was born, and so she took her place in the kitchen with *mamm.*

Wishing she could work the stove or sew a quilt square that actually looked like a square, Grace felt she'd missed out on a lot of time with her *mamm.* But she certainly made up for it with time spent caring for little Jonah. He was her favorite sibling, even though she would never admit it. At twelve, Jonah had become fun to be around, and Grace was as proud as a *mamm* would be at the responsible young man he'd become.

"*Mamm* and I made the breakfast, so don't worry about it," Lilly put her digs in.

Grace narrowed her eyes at the girl. "I'm not in the mood for this today, Lilly, I'm warning you!"

"You seem to be in quite the mood today," her younger sister said.

It was true. Today was the day she was to give Seth Yoder her answer.

She'd promised.

But after hearing the news her parents had shared, she knew she just couldn't go through with it.

Not now.

How could she possibly marry Seth when she didn't feel she had anything to offer him? She didn’t even know who she was. Her *mamm* had admitted to her that her *daed* was not her father. There was a whole other world, an *Englisch* world, which she'd had no idea existed for her.

Perhaps if her *mamm* had given her more time to learn the news surrounding her birth. Maybe then she would be more used to the idea and would be ready to marry Seth. But the way she felt now, there was no way she was ready to marry and settle down. It just wouldn't be fair to Seth. At least that's what she was telling herself at the moment.

"We took care of everything this morning," Lilly continued. "While you were out in the barn playing with the kittens."

I'm sorry my life isn't perfect like yours, Grace thought, trying to choke down tears that threatened to spill from her eyes.

She had to get out of the kitchen.

Had to get out of the house.

Had to get out of the community.

She couldn't take it anymore.

Grace was out the kitchen door before her *mamm* could stop her. Anna had seen the look on her daughter's face, but felt powerless to keep from breaking down herself, and that would not be wise in front of the other children.

Grace reached the barn out of breath, her tears flowing to rich, uncontrollable sobs. She knew it was only a matter of time before her *mamm* came after her, but right now she didn't want to be around her. She felt betrayed.

The wind blew snow into the barn as her *mamm* entered through the large door. Anna closed the space between them, attempting to hug Grace, but she shrugged the woman away.

"I didn't mean to hurt you," her *mamm* offered.

"Would you have kept this secret from me my entire life if I hadn't found that little hat?"

"I don't know," her mother admitted. "But I realize now we should have told you sooner."

"I'm not certain if it would be worse never knowing or being told sooner in life. All I know is that I can't face any of you right now. Can I go for a visit with your *Aenti* Sadie?"

It was all she could think of, but Grace needed to put some distance between her and her *mamm*.

Anna nodded. "That might be for the best. Pack a bag and I'll have your *daed* hitch up the buggy and drive you."

Relief washed over Grace as her *mamm* left the barn to search out her *daed*.

Her *daed*.

Funny how foreign that suddenly felt to her.

CHAPTER 16

Grace rode quietly next to her *daed* in the buggy. What was she to say to him? There was nothing either of them could say. He wasn't her father, and that was that. There was no changing it. There was no stopping it. Once that sort of thing was heard, it wasn't something you could undo, no matter what.

Grace certainly wished she could.

She wished more than anything that the conversation would've been one of those where she daydreamed instead of listening to her parents. She'd done it so often there was no telling how many things she'd missed over the course of her lifetime. But this particular thing, she hadn't missed. She wished someone would take it back.

More than anything, she wished it was all a bad dream and someone would tell her that it just wasn't true. For now, Grace couldn't get to her *aenti's haus* fast enough. The silence between her and her *daed* was maddening. One thing was certain, Grace knew things would never be the same between them.

As they pulled onto the city street, Grace looked mindlessly into the windows of the *Englisch* shops. Normally, she would keep her eyes forward, as was proper and expected, but today she felt compelled to explore her *Englisch* side.

Grace had never had any interest in the *Englisch* world, but now it seemed, she was more intrigued than ever. Quite possibly she'd gained a new feeling of freedom in all of this, or perhaps it was the *Englisch* blood running through her veins that was tempting her. Either way, Grace knew she would never look at the world around her the same ever again.

She couldn't help but think how different this visit would be with *Aenti* Sadie. Her *aenti* lived in the heart of downtown in one of the historic homes. She'd never married and never had any children of her own. Being a school teacher for over forty years, she'd always said that her students were her children. Having left the community to pursue a higher education, Grace knew how fortunate she was that her family wasn't required to shun her. As a child, Grace had loved visiting the woman in the summers and spending countless warm afternoons on her wraparound porch snapping beans from the garden and sipping fresh lemonade.

There was no doubt this visit would be nothing like those.

As they rounded the corner in town, Grace's eyes latched onto something that made her heart drop to her shoes. The red jacket and blond hair were the first things to grab her attention. When she set her gaze upon the young woman's face, it was like looking in the mirror.

How could this be?

Was it possible the young woman was related to Grace?

She had to know.

"Stop the buggy," Grace hollered suddenly.

"What's wrong?"

"I'd like to pick up some chamomile tea for *Aenti* Sadie."

It was the first thing that came to her mind, but she had to feed her curiosity over this no matter what.

"Alright," he agreed. "I suppose I could drop you off and go to the hardware store for some nails."

Even if he wasn't her father, there was one thing Grace knew about Jacob Fisher; he was a very agreeable man. She was grateful for that at the moment as she focused her gaze on the young woman standing in the doorway of the specialty shop she was headed for.

"I'll be back in a few minutes," Jacob said, handing her a few dollars from his pocket.

Grace snatched the money from his hands and nodded, and then crossed the freshly-plowed street. At the curb, she narrowly escaped a pothole filled with slush, and then had to conquer the embankment of snow created by the plows. As she made her way over the mound of dirty ice and snow, Grace lost sight of the young woman. When she reached the shoveled walkway, the red-coated woman was nowhere in sight.

Panic filled her.

She needed to find the young woman like she needed her next breath.

The jingling of bells from the bookstore startled Grace and caused her to duck inside the doorway of The Tea Kettle, where she intended to pick up the chamomile tea for her *aenti.*

Out of the corner of her eye, Grace spotted the red jacket and blond hair. Heading the opposite direction, Grace followed her at a distance.

What was she doing?

What would she say if she caught up to the girl, and how would she react to being followed. Grace thought she must seem crazy, but at the moment, she had to admit she felt pretty out-of-sorts.

The young woman turned suddenly into the doorway of the building at the end of the block. By the time Grace reached the building, the young woman had entered through a glass door of an upscale building. Grace watched the young woman walk up a wide, marbled staircase and put a key into the door at the top of the stairs. On the inside wall where Grace stood, two fancy brass mailboxes adorned the marble wall. One boasted the name of an attorney—the other box had the name Mercy Pritchard etched on a brass plate.

Now she knew where the would-be relative lived and what her name was. She would have to return after she'd settled in at her *aenti's haus* so she could meet the young woman and discover why it was that they looked so much alike they could practically be twins. The thought of it filled her with both exhilaration and fear, but at least she was feeling something other than anger at the moment, and that was a good thing.

CHAPTER 17

"I'll be back in a week to pick you up," her *daed* said.

Grace looked at him and forced a weak smile as he handed her bag to her. She felt like she was about to cry, but she didn't want to break down in front of her *daed.*

He pulled her toward him and hugged her. "I hope you find the answers you're looking for," he said as he released her from his embrace.

"*Danki*," was all she could say without crying.

Grace took her bag of meager belongings and trudged up the steps to her *aenti's haus*. Though she was struggling, she was looking forward to her visit because the best thing about *Aenti* Sadie was that Grace knew she could tell her anything and she wouldn't be judged. She wouldn't even have to talk if she didn't want to, because *Aenti* Sadie wouldn't make her. They could sit and talk about nothing, and it would mean more to Grace than having a whole roomful of people to talk to. Being apart from the community, her *aenti* understood things. She understood things that even Grace's own *mamm* didn't understand.

Grace pounded on the heavy door with the butt of her hand because she knew her *aenti* wouldn't hear it otherwise. The older woman opened the door with a cheerful welcome as always, but her expression dropped when she saw Grace's sad face. *Aenti* Sadie looked beyond Grace to Jacob, who was standing outside the buggy at the road. He threw her a wave before climbing back in the buggy and riding away.

Aenti Sadie focused on Grace. "Well, come in out of the cold," she said.

Grace went inside and set her bag down, then *Aenti* Sadie pulled her into a hug. No sooner did she sink into the safety of the older woman's arms than she begin to sob.

"It can't be that bad, can it? They didn't disown you, did they?" *Aenti* Sadie asked.

Grace sobbed even harder. "It feels like it."

"Well, the way your *daed* dropped you off, I thought something was up. Let's get some hot cocoa into you and get you by the fire so you can get warmed up, and then we'll talk if you want to," *Aenti* Sadie offered.

Grace nodded as she followed the older woman into the kitchen. If there was a solution to be found, she knew her *Aenti* Sadie would help her find it. And at the end of the day, the older woman would tuck her into a stack of hand-stitched quilts and wish her sweet dreams. The only thing that would wake her would be the sweet smell of *Aenti* Sadie's famous pecan rolls she would surely bake for the morning meal.

Perhaps this visit would turn out to be more like a vacation. She could certainly use a vacation from reality right now. But one thing still weighed heavily on Grace's mind.

Who was her mysterious look-alike in the red coat, and how was she to approach her?

Grace woke up just the way she hoped she would; smelling breakfast. The only time she ever slept in was when she stayed with *Aenti* Sadie.

At home, she would have been up for at least two hours already and had the cow milked, the chickens fed, eggs gathered, and all their many pets fed and watered. In summer, she'd have berries picked and herbs gathered to make sun tea for the afternoon.

At *Aenti* Sadie's *haus,* time slowed almost to a standstill. Sure, there were chores to be done, but not like on the farm. These chores, such as shoveling the walk or sweeping the front porch, or even washing dishes, could be done any time of the day, and did not require early rising. Living in town, her *aenti* only had enough room in her yard for a small garden. Though it was big enough to yield enough food to eat from over the summer, she didn't usually have enough to put up for winter months.

Normally, Grace's *mamm* would bring home-canned vegetables and fruits when they came for a visit, but they'd just brought her a large batch recently at their Christmas visit, and she was most likely not in need just yet. She imagined her *daed*—Jacob would bring a supply when he returned in a week to pick her back up and take her home as promised.

Home…

The way Grace felt right now, she didn't ever want to go home. She hadn't even told Seth she was leaving. She couldn't tell him she was going without giving him an answer to his proposal. He'd have wanted an answer, and Grace just could not give that to him right now. She'd been a coward, that was for sure and for certain, but she wasn't ready for him to put her on the spot. She would have felt obligated to give him an answer of yes, and right now she wasn't certain she felt that way. It had nothing to do with him; she certainly cared about him. It had everything to do with her broken family life. How could she begin a family with Seth when she had none of her own at the moment?

Grace sniffed the air.

Pecan rolls were her favorite, and her *aenti's* were the best by far. She wished she could make them herself, but she was so inept when it came to domestic duties. Everything she tried to make she burned, or it turned out too dry. She even feared her poor Seth would die of starvation if he married her.

Ahhh, Seth.

She missed him.

She definitely missed him. That she was sure of. But would it be fair to marry him when she wasn't sure of herself? No, it was best she wait until she could make some sense of her life.

She would start by finding out who her *twin* was, and how it was they looked so much alike. She almost wondered if there was more to the story that her parents hadn't shared with her. Was it possible her *mamm* had more than one baby that day? She pushed down such a thought, feeling it disrespected her *mamm* to think that she would keep one child and give away another. But she *did* give Grace away in the beginning…was it possible she'd given away two?

It was just too absurd an idea to even entertain.

But how could she explain the girl that looked almost identical to her, who seemed to be the same age as Grace herself? There had to be a logical explanation for it, and she was determined to find out the truth—even if it caused her and her family more anguish. The truth was always best—except maybe in this case.

I can certainly hope for such a thing, Grace thought.

She rose from the warmth of the quilts and pushed her feet into a pair of slippers, knowing she wasn't required to dress for the morning meal at her *aenti's haus.* Lazy mornings were a luxury at this home, and Grace welcomed it. Now retired, *Aenti* Sadie had all the time in the world to spoil Grace, and it was exactly what she needed most at the moment.

In the kitchen, her *aenti* greeted her warmly with a cup of hot cocoa and a warm plate of gooey goodness, all topped with the most pecans one could fit on top of a roll. Her mouth watered, but she reached up and gave her *aenti* a lengthy hug before sitting down to the best breakfast in the world.

"I knew the smell of my pecan rolls would get you up," her *aenti* said with a smile.

Grace wanted to tell her of her worries about the young woman she'd seen in town yesterday, but she decided it was best to wait until she knew more herself before she shared it with the woman. She'd made herself a promise that she would not jump to any more conclusions, and that she would wait to find out the real answers to the mystery involving the young woman.

In the meantime, she would enjoy her time with her *aenti,* and relish the slowness of the time spent with her.

She bit into the roll, and her taste-buds made her forget her troubles instantly—even if only for a minute.

"It wouldn't be the same here without these," Grace said with a smile.

"I'm getting on in years, though," her *aenti* said. "And I think you should learn how to make these for yourself. You will make your new husband happy, and many a *kinner.*"

Grace's expression fell. "*Ach,* I'm not so certain that marriage is in my future just yet.

Besides, you know what a *dummkopf* I am in the kitchen."

Her *aenti* reached across the table and patted Grace's hand. "You and Seth will figure it out, but like I told you last night; you need to sit down and really talk to him. He is to be your husband, which means you can tell him anything. If you can't, then he is not the one for you.

As for baking these pecan rolls, there is a simple and easy secret to cooking, and I will teach you all you need to know to be a successful *fraa.*"

Grace smiled at her *aenti,* knowing the woman would do anything for her.

CHAPTER 18

Grace walked around the corner toward the building where she'd seen the young woman the day before, hoping to meet her, or at the very least, to catch another glimpse of her. As distraught as she was, Grace hoped her mind had simply been playing tricks on her. If not, she would soon find out.

She was grateful her *aenti* didn't question her when she left the *haus.* At home, she would have been interrogated by Lilly, and the girl would have made such a fuss that her *mamm* would have ended up getting involved needlessly. Then the *real* questions would have started. *Aenti* Sadie had never been as strict with Grace as her parents had been. She supposed a lot of it had to do with the *Ordnung,* which *Aenti* Sadie was no longer a part of. But mostly, she felt her *aenti* trusted her more than her parents did, even though she'd never given them reason not to trust her.

As for her courtship with Seth, that is where the real trust issues unfolded, since her parents had been far stricter than the community, but she supposed it all made sense now. Her *mamm* was most likely trying to prevent her from repeating the same mistake she'd made at Grace's age. She'd been raised in an atmosphere so strict it was almost stifling. But with *Aenti* Sadie, she had the freedom to explore, and that is exactly what she needed right now.

As she neared the building, Grace tried her best to rehearse what she might say to *Mercy,* but what could she say? Anything she would say would make her look crazy—and not the fun kind of crazy—the scary kind!

Before she realized, the young woman came bustling through the glass door of the building and ran smack into Grace. They both stood there staring at one another as though looking at their own reflection. Aside from the difference in clothing, and Grace's hair being bound tightly behind her *kapp,* they had absolute identical features, right down to the freckles on their noses. Though the young woman in the red coat wore a bit of makeup, the freckles could still be seen.

Neither girl moved.

Grace didn't dare breathe.

Time seemed to stand still.

Even the snow seemed to hover in mid-air, the earth unmoving, and deafeningly quiet.

"*Oh my-gosh*, you must be Grace," the other girl burst out. "I've been wanting to meet you forever!"

"How—how do you know who I am?" Grace managed to spit out.

"From the letters your mother sent to my father—he's actually *your* dad too! I'm Mercy, and we're sisters!"

She pulled Grace into a hug, but Grace couldn't seem to get her arms to work. She couldn't move. Couldn't hug the girl back. She couldn't think.

So it was all true.

It wasn't just a bad dream.

She had a different *father*—who was an *Englischer*—and a *schweschder* too!

"*Oh my-gosh.* You didn't know anything about me, did you?"

"*Ach,* I only just found out I have a different *daed* two days ago."

Judging by Mercy's expression, Grace knew her accent must be coming out too thick for the girl to understand her. She had a tendency to do that when she was nervous. Usually it happened when she was in town having to deal directly with *Englischers.* She knew they expected it, which made it harder for Grace to avoid for some reason.

When Mercy's expression changed, Grace knew what she'd said finally registered.

"I'm sorry. *Girl*—you must be in shock. Let's go across the street and sit at the coffee shop and grab a cup of coffee."

"*Ach, mei mamm* won't let me drink *kaffi,*" Grace said, fumbling over the words.

"Well, I don't see your momma anywhere near here, so I'm gonna treat my sister to a cup of coffee!"

Mercy pulled Grace's arm into the fold of hers and led her across the street like cattle. Grace was still in too much shock to resist the strong-willed young woman.

They crossed the slushy street, dodging cars, while Grace followed like a lost lamb. When they entered the coffee shop, Grace inhaled. It smelled just like her *mamm's* kitchen in the afternoon when the woman would put on a fresh pot of *kaffi* and baked cinnamon rolls for her *daed.*

They stepped up to the counter and Mercy took over when the young woman stepped up to the other side of the counter to take their order. She stared at the two of them, probably making mental notes of their likenesses, and polar opposite attire. It made Grace feel uncomfortable to be scrutinized this way. She was used to stares when she was around *Englischers,* but this was somehow different. Different because she was standing next to an *Englischer* who looked just like her.

Mercy turned to Grace. "I'm guessing you've never been here before?"

Grace shook her head.

"Then I'll order you the same thing I always get. You will like it because it's sweet and doesn't taste like coffee at all, and if you've never had coffee before, this will make you *love* it!"

Grace made a mental note of how overly expressive Mercy was when she talked and wondered if she was only this way because she, too, was nervous.

Mercy turned her attention back to the young woman standing behind the counter, confusion marring her reflection.

"We'll have two Tall, one-and-a-half-shot, five-pump, white mocha, with whip."

What did she just say?

Grace could no more process Mercy's order than she could process the fact she was standing in a coffee shop with the girl.

Mercy ushered them to the other end of the counter under a sign that read: *Pick up order here.* After a lot of whirring and swishing and sputtering, steam puffing up from every machine, the young woman handed them two cups with white lids, a small slit in the top where steam billowed out. Mercy grabbed both cups and gestured toward a table in the corner with odd furniture that looked mildly uncomfortable, yet functional.

Grace was wrong. The oversized chair was quite comfortable. Mercy handed her the beverage and showed her how to *sip* it through the slit, but warned her to sip slowly so she didn't burn her tongue.

"If you burn your tongue, it will ruin the flavor, and you will probably like the sweetness of this drink. I have them put in five pumps of the flavoring so it's more flavor than coffee taste cuz I can't stand the bitter taste of coffee."

Grace tried the beverage, sipping it the way Mercy instructed. It was quite tasty, she had to admit. No wonder her *mamm* didn't want her to drink this stuff. It was *gut!*

She was grateful for the distraction that involved keeping her hands occupied with holding the warm cup against her cold hands, and for the slow sipping to keep her from having to speak, lest she say something stupid.

She watched Mercy take off her hat, her smooth blond hair looking just the way hers did when she pulled it down at night before bed. Aside from the fact Mercy's hair was about four inches shorter than Grace's, and she wore a little makeup, she thought to herself that quite possibly, even her own *mamm* wouldn't be able to tell the two of them apart.

CHAPTER 19

"Tell me more about these letters *mei mamm* wrote to your *daed,*" Grace said as she set her half-empty cup down on the odd-shaped table in front of her. She rested her forearms on the table and fumbled with her cup to keep her hands occupied. She was almost too afraid to hear Mercy's explanation, but more than that, she was fighting anger over the fact her *mamm* had told her nothing of the letters. She hadn't even told Grace what her father's name was.

She was curious to find out why her *mamm* had written the letters, and wondered if her *daed*—Jacob knew about them. Probably her biggest question was why her *real daed* never wanted to meet her if he knew about her.

"I only know about them because I have a tendency to go through my father's desk in his office at his home where I grew up with him. The first letter was rather personal, and you should probably talk to your mother about that one. I know she'd mentioned being shunned and giving you up to another family to avoid that. It was a very sad letter. I think my father assumed she gave you up for adoption because there wasn't another letter until you turned eighteen years old and she said that you had become an adult, and he could see you if he wanted to."

"That was only a few years ago!" Grace shrieked.

Her cheeks turned pink as the other customers of the coffee shop stopped what they were doing and stared at her with furrowed eyebrows. They all seemed to be working on computers or reading, and her outburst had obviously disturbed them.

"That was not that long ago!" she repeated in a whisper. "He didn't come to see me."

"Actually, he did," Mercy said. "He attended some barn-raising picnic, and you were there, but too busy with a boyfriend to notice he was there."

"How do you know all of this?" Grace asked angrily.

Mercy shrugged. "I make it my business to know my father's business."

"Why didn't you come with him that day?"

Mercy smiled and winked at Grace. "I was going through a selfish phase then. But now that I'm more mature and over all of that, I've wanted to meet you for a while. I always wanted a sister."

"I have two of them," Grace complained with a roll of her eyes. "But it's not all that great. Lilly is so rude to me and gets me in trouble all the time. Plus she makes me look bad at everything because she's so *gut*—good at everything. Then there's Becca, who never talks. She keeps to herself. But Jonah, *mei* little *bruder*—brother, he's the best! We have a lot of fun. He has this rock collection, and we look for rocks at the creek every chance we get. He's so cute, he even gives them names."

"I'm actually an only child—except for you," Mercy said, sadness clouding her eyes. "My mother died giving birth to me, so my father was *stuck* with me. If it hadn't been for the cooks and the housekeeper, I probably would not have had even the slightest bit of a normal childhood. They taught me to cook and sew, and all the things a mother would show me how to do, I suppose. I guess because I never knew her, I didn't really miss having a mother. How are you with your parents?"

Grace shrugged. "They are kind, but I don't spend a lot of time with them. Lilly makes certain I don't get near *mei mudder*—mother, because she's always boasting about how she can cook better than I can, and she's right, so I do a lot of chores with Jonah and stay out of the kitchen with the two of them. There is always so much to be done on the farm that there isn't much time left at the end of the day, but *mei daed*—father, always reads to us after we have our evening meal. I've tried to sew and cook, but I'm clumsy at it."

"Maybe I should go in your place and show your sister up for the know-it-all she is!"

Grace laughed, but maybe Mercy had something there. Perhaps, just maybe, that wasn't such a bad idea.

CHAPTER 20

Grace rolled out of her bed, squinting at the sunlight coming in the window, unable to hold her head upright without it pounding. She groaned as she stuffed her feet into her slippers and shuffled down the hall, hoping she could make it down the stairs without falling over. She couldn't ever remember having a headache this bad, and it was worrying her.

She staggered into the kitchen, tying to see well enough through the slit in her eyes to keep from bumping into the furniture. She hoped a glass of water would help this headache the same as it helped smaller ones she'd experienced over the years.

Her *aenti* took one look at her and steered her to a chair. Easing her down on the chair, Grace winced and groaned despite how careful her *aenti* was being.

"You got home pretty late last night, Grace. Please tell me you weren't drinking alcohol."

She groaned again and laid her head down on the table. "Of course not," Grace said letting out a loud groan. "The only thing I had to drink yesterday was a big cup of *kaffi* at the *kaffi* shop."

Aenti Sadie let out a guffaw as she crossed to the stove and poured a cup of *kaffi*.

"What is so funny about drinking *kaffi?* Or was that laughter more from relief that I wasn't out being rebellious?"

She handed Grace the cup. "Here, drink this. It will make your head stop hurting. I was laughing because it seems like you've got yourself a simple *kaffi* headache!"

"This isn't a simple headache," Grace whined. "It feels like my head is going to split open and my brain is gonna fall out!"

"Is this your first time having *kaffi*?" *Aenti* Sadie asked.

"*Jah*," Grace answered.

"Well now you understand why your *mamm* always told you no. She was trying to spare you all this pain. But now that you've gone and had your first cup, you will have to keep drinking it to keep the headache away."

Grace tipped her head up toward her *aenti*, trying to keep from vomiting. "You mean I'm gonna feel like this every morning?"

Her *aenti* laughed. "Not if you make sure you get a cup of *kaffi* bright and early every morning."

Grace took another gulp of the bitter brew her *aenti* Sadie had brought her, realizing her headache was easing up. "So this is what my *mamm* meant when she said I'd get hooked on *kaffi*."

"I'm afraid you're hooked now unless you can wean yourself from it, but that might take a few days."

"But I liked that *kaffi*," Grace said, shuddering from the bitterness of her *aenti's kaffi*. "Not this stuff. I don't mean any disrespect *Aenti*, but this stuff is awful."

The woman laughed. "That's probably because the girl behind the counter at the *kaffi* shop sold you their most flavorful *kaffi,* that it probably didn't taste anything like the real stuff. When that shop first opened, I went for a cup just out of curiosity of how a cup of *kaffi* could cost so much, and I had the same experience. It kept me coming back for a few days just for the taste, but in the end I realized I could make it at home and have it taste *almost* as *gut*."

She took Grace's cup over to the counter and mixed in a few things, and then handed it back to her.

Grace took a sip and smiled. "*Jah,* that is much better. How did you get it to taste like that?"

Her *aenti* walked back to the counter and held up a bottle of clear liquid. "I got this at the same shop in town where you buy my chamomile tea. It's a flavored syrup. Mix it with a little cream and your *kaffi* tastes almost as *gut* as if it came from that fancy shop."

Grace nodded. "It's close to the same, but not quite. Perhaps you should get one of those fancy machines that makes all the noise like they have."

"I think that makes the *kaffi* a little too strong, so I'll stick to this syrup and cream. And when I want the really *gut* stuff, I'll indulge myself at the fancy *kaffi* shop. I usually go in there and sit once a month."

Grace let a brief giggle escape her lips, but quickly put her hand to her head from the dull ache that still clung to her. Laughing somehow made it worse, but she couldn't help but think how her *aenti* certainly was full of fun surprises.

CHAPTER 21

Grace entered the coffee shop and immediately spotted Mercy's red coat and long blonde hair. The girl didn't have to be facing her for Grace to recognize her. She was already standing in line to order a cup of the addictive brew and turned around to signal Grace to join her.

"I had no idea this stuff was so addictive," Grace whispered. "I woke up with the worst headache I've ever had."

Mercy turned to her sister, a look of surprise filling her expression. "That wasn't your *first* cup of coffee, was it?"

Grace nodded slowly, embarrassment pinking up her cheeks. "*Jah,* it was."

"Wow, you really do live a sheltered life, don't you?"

"That's really not such a bad thing," Grace said in her defense.

Mercy rolled her eyes and smiled.

They stepped up to the counter, and once again, Mercy ordered for the two of them.

"Do you want me to get us a table?" Grace suggested, "It's getting kind of crowded."

"No, I thought we could go across the street and I could show you my place. My—*our* dad just gave me the building for my twenty-first birthday, and I'm renting the downstairs to a really hot young attorney. He came with the building!"

Grace nodded, trying to keep up with Mercy's meaning to what she was saying.

"When was your birthday?"

"Just last week on February first," Mercy answered as she grabbed both cups of coffee and handed one to Grace.

"That makes us only about a month apart. I just turned twenty-one on Christmas day!"

Mercy almost choked on her coffee. "Our dad didn't waste any time getting with my mom after being with *your* mom, did he?"

"I suppose he didn't," Grace agreed quietly as they left the coffee shop.

"I suppose it's strange to think that both our moms got pregnant as teenagers by the same guy."

"Not so strange when you see how much we look alike," Grace said.

"But we do both look exactly like my—*our* dad."

Grace couldn't imagine committing such a scandalous act, but she supposed her own *mamm* had been a party to their father's reckless way of life. What had she been thinking? She'd admitted that she'd been drinking alcohol the night Grace was conceived, and that if she hadn't, Grace would likely not be here. She didn't know whether to be grateful for the beer her *mamm* had consumed, or ashamed of her for indulging in such carelessness. She decided she was grateful, even though she didn't understand. It certainly put an unsavory image of her *mamm* in her mind—an image she would do most anything to get rid of.

Grace made up her mind right then that the most rebellious thing she would do would be drinking the coffee. She would make sure she learned from her *mamm's* mistakes and keep herself pure with Seth until they were married—if she decided to accept his proposal.

They were to be married at the end of March, so she didn't have much time to keep putting off answering him. She should have given him an answer in November when he'd first asked, but for some reason, she felt the need for more time to think. After all, they'd only been seeing each other less than a year, and Grace worried it was too soon to determine if they were right enough to last a lifetime. She cared for him, there was no question there, but she was still young, and had obviously not experienced much outside the community. Before Seth, she had dated Simon, until his family had left the community abruptly. She had loved Simon.

Perhaps a change would be good. Maybe Mercy would consider letting her stay with her for a while. The only problem would be getting around her parents. They might think she was running off and wouldn't return to the community to be baptized, even though she was leaning toward skipping her baptism.

She wouldn't be shunned, but she would be like *Aenti* Sadie—apart from them. Did she want that? Perhaps not, but she wasn't certain she wanted to go back at the end of the week when her *daed* came for her either.

When they entered the shelter of Mercy's building, Grace was grateful to be out of the wind and snow. She followed Mercy up the grand stairway and into an even grander apartment that was bigger than her family's house.

One large room with brick walls consisted of a living room with the largest television Grace had ever seen, a sitting area with a baby grand piano, an eating area that adjoined the kitchen that was separated by a breakfast bar. A leather sofa and two blue and white striped arm chairs with pretty, floral pillows looked so inviting, Grace felt she could sink into the space and not come out for a while.

Mercy offered to take Grace's wool coat, and she declined with a shiver despite the hot coffee in her hand.

"You must be freezing in that dress, Grace. Do you want to borrow a pair of jeans?"

Grace looked at her with unsureness in her eyes. "I'll be fine. I'm used to wearing the dress. Besides, I have on warm stockings."

"Have you ever worn a pair of pants in your life, Grace?"

She shook her head.

Mercy smiled mischievously. "Oh my-gosh, you don't know what you're missing. Humor me and try on a pair."

Mercy disappeared into another room before Grace could protest. She came back out within minutes with a few pairs of jeans and tops, and shoved them toward Grace. "The bathroom is in there."

Grace took them, intending only to humor Mercy. She felt awkward taking the items, but she would indulge her sister. She flipped on the light of the bathroom and entered slowly, her eyes wide and her heart yearning for such a luxurious room of her own. A round, tufted stool sat under the counter where the sink was, a hand-carved frame enclosed a mirror the length of one wall. In the center, a large, round bathtub big enough to bathe a horse beckoned her to take a swim in it. A tall door with a glass transom enclosed the toilet.

She giggled.

The toilet has its own room!

She walked up to the bathtub, noting that the rim was the same height as her waist. She had no idea they made a tub that large. The one at her family's home was so small Grace's feet touched the end when she sat in it and the height didn't even reach her knees when she stood next to it.

She could live here and be spoiled. Suddenly she wondered if her *real daed* would shower her with such a gift as this. Would she accept it if he did?

Perhaps…just maybe.

CHAPTER 22

Grace walked out of the bathroom feeling very awkward in Mercy’s clothing. "They don't fit," she complained. "They're way too tight as you can see."

Mercy giggled. "They're supposed to be tight, Grace. They hug you in all the right places, and that's what makes them look good."

Grace thought for certain that would get her out of having to wear the clothes, but Mercy wouldn’t hear of it. She didn’t see how any woman would choose to wear this tight stuff on purpose.

It was uncomfortable.

Her dresses were comfortable *and* practical. She could bend and stoop and move about freely as she did her chores, and when she ate, her dresses never pinched her waist.

"Are they supposed to pinch you when you sit down?"

"Of course they are, Grace."

Fidgeting in the chair that also wasn't as comfortable as it looked, Grace pulled at a belt-loop, hoping it would give her some relief. "Why don't you just buy a bigger size?"

"They would be baggy, and that would look awful!"

"But they would be comfortable," Grace said with a giggle.

Mercy shook her head. "They aren't supposed to be comfortable. They're just supposed to look nice."

"Sort of like this chair," Grace complained as she stood up.

"Those chairs are not comfortable at all," Mercy agreed.

"Then why do you have them?"

Mercy laughed a little. "Because they look so cute in my new place!"

"You've got me there. They do look nice—the pants too. But just don't expect me to wear these jeans out in public."

"The outfit is missing something," Mercy said. "Come with me."

Grace followed her sister into the bathroom where Mercy began to unpin her hair. "I'm sure you're not supposed to take your hair down, but I want to compare it to mine."

Once her hair was unwound, Grace took the hairbrush and untangled the tendrils that were at least four inches longer than Mercy's.

"With a little bit of mascara and a little bit of lip gloss, you would look exactly like me."

Grace held up the ends of her hair. "Except for this. My hair is longer."

"We can fix that," Mercy said with a smile.

Grace pulled her hair to one side and twisted it. "I can't cut my hair!"

"Why not?"

"We aren't really supposed to, but more than that, I've never cut my hair before."

Mercy picked up the bottom of her hair to examine it. "It looks like you've trimmed the ends. They're way too smooth to never be trimmed."

Grace shook her head. "I put coconut oil or olive oil on the ends to keep it smooth. I've never trimmed my hair before."

"I've heard of that, but never thought it would make such a difference." She ran her fingers down her sister's hair. "I wish my hair was this smooth."

"We can go to the store tomorrow and get some for you, and I'll show you how much to use. It will help your hair to grow too."

"Then no one would be able to tell us apart," Mercy said excitedly. "We could trade places and no one would know the difference."

Grace giggled. "*Mei mamm* would know it wasn't me."

"Do you want to make a friendly bet on it? I've been taking acting classes, and I could fool anyone. I could even fool your *mamm* into thinking I was you, for sure and for certain."

Grace's eyes grew wide. "You sounded just like me!"

Excitement filled her at the thought of trading places with Mercy. It might just work.

CHAPTER 23

"Hold still, Grace," Mercy demanded. "Or it will turn out crooked."

Grace couldn't help but whine and fidget. She didn't like the idea of cutting her hair, but she knew it was the only way they would be able to pull off their scheme. They'd spent the last four days rehearsing each other's lives to the point there would be no mistakes—right down to Mercy's put-on accent.

"I've changed my mind!" Grace squealed.

"It's too late. I'm half way done."

Grace looked up into the mirror. She'd purposely closed her eyes in the beginning, knowing that if she saw the first snip she'd have freaked out. But it seemed that keeping her eyes closed was not enough. Hearing the snipping of the shears and feeling the hair brush against her arm as it fell to the bathroom floor was enough to send her into a dramatic tailspin.

"What if I'm shunned for this?"

"Grace, get a hold of yourself. You always have your hair pinned back, so how would anyone except me and you ever know that you've cut your hair?"

"That *you* cut my hair," Grace corrected her.

"Okay, that I cut your hair! If you need me to take the blame, then I can accept that. But just remember whose idea this was in the first place."

"Yours!" Grace said with a nervous giggle.

"Okay. I can see how this is gonna go. I'll take the blame for all of it. But only if you let me put Lilly in her place—let me show her that *you* can cook and sew just as good as she can, if not better."

Grace shook her head furiously. "*Nee*-no! Remember, we talked about this. You have to act as much like me as possible or *mei mamm* will know it's not me. Stay out of the kitchen, don't talk too much, and remember to tell Seth you—I can't see him for a week, and you'll give him your answer then."

"This may be none of my business, but it seems to me that if you have taken all this time to give the guy an answer to his proposal, it might just be that you don't want to marry him."

Grace pursed her lips and blew at the hair that covered her eyes. "You're right about it not being any of your business, but I have to figure out how to handle the proposal from Seth in my own way in my own time."

"What was the other guy's name again?"

"You mean Simon Bontrager? I haven't seen him in almost a year. He somehow found out that Seth told everyone we were betrothed before I even gave him an answer, and so he stopped talking to me. It doesn't matter anyway because *mei daed* never approved of Simon. His parents ran off and left the community and the Amish way of life, so *mei daed* thought he would not make a *gut* match for me. He was worried Simon would take me away from the community the way his *daed* did."

"If you had to choose today which one you wanted, and you didn't have to take into consideration what your parents thought or what they wanted—who would *you* choose?"

Grace's expression fell. "Seth is the better choice. I would have an easier life with him—without *mei vadder* and *mudder* putting doubt in my mind with their opinions."

"Sounds to me like you would prefer Simon, but don't want to upset your family. Why marry a man you don't love just because he's the *better* match? If you're not happy, then he isn't the better choice."

"I do love Seth—at least I think I do," Grace said in her defense. "A friendship sort of love, but it's enough to build on. Over time, I will love him more and more."

Mercy raised an eyebrow. "Or resent him because you don't love him enough to make up for the strong *friendship* you have."

"I am going to marry Seth, and we will be happy. I just have to prepare myself for a life with him—that's all."

"I've never been in love," Mercy admitted. "But it seems that if you really loved Seth, you wouldn't have to think about *if* you want to marry him, or why he's the best choice. If you loved him enough to marry him, that would be all you could think about, and you wouldn't be able to wait until you were married. You would be so filled with passion for him that you would be counting the hours and the minutes until you could be his wife!"

Grace combed out her hair and put a little bit of coconut oil on the ends. The more distance she put between her and Seth, the more she was beginning to see he may not be the one for her. Mercy had certainly given her something to think about. Only problem was, it was Simon whom she couldn't get out of her mind—not Seth.

CHAPTER 24

"Tell *daed* to pick me up at the *kaffi* shop," Grace said as she hugged her *aenti.* "I'm going to miss you."

"Are you sure you don't want me to go with you?"

Grace shook her head. "This is something I have to do by myself."

Her *aenti* gave her an affectionate squeeze. "I understand. I'm going to miss you. Make sure you send me an invitation to your wedding—if you decided to marry him—or anyone else."

Grace giggled. "I will. I promise. *Danki* for letting me stay. I really needed this trip. I think it did more for me than I could have ever imagined."

Her *aenti* smiled. "I'm glad I could help. I love you, Grace."

"I love you too."

Grace picked up her bag and walked out into the snowy day. She didn't want to walk in the crisp morning air, but it would be easier to change places with Mercy. Her *daed* would be none the wiser when he showed up and picked up Mercy instead of Grace. Her *aenti* would certainly notice if her *twin* showed up at the house and switched places with her to go *home.* Thankfully, for now, Grace would be able to avoid home for a little while longer—thanks to Mercy agreeing to take her place.

Grace had to admit that she worried about how a city girl like Mercy would fare on the farm, but she assured her she could handle it since she'd had summers with her mother's parents on a farm all her growing years.

As she rounded the corner toward the coffee shop, Mercy was waiting for her outside.

"Hurry," she called to Grace. "We won't have much time to go over last-minute details if we don't hurry and change our clothes."

Grace quickened her pace as best she could without slipping on the fresh snow that blanketed the sidewalk. When she reached the coffee shop, she followed Mercy into the bathroom where they began the exchange.

"I went to the store last night and picked up the kind of underwear you said you wore so that when it was wash-day, your *mamm* wouldn't suspect anything if there were not any of your things there for the clothesline. You really hang laundry in this cold weather?"

"We have lines in the basement that we use in winter, but the sheets do go outside—they just smell better—once you knock the ice off of them!"

"Tell me you're kidding," Mercy begged.

"It's only for one week," Grace said with a giggle. "Surely you can survive *one* wash-day at *mei haus!* By the time I get back, you will think your own life is not so boring after all."

Grace suspected that the reason Mercy agreed to make the exchange was not a simple matter of boredom with her own life as she'd claimed, but more that she craved a family life that she'd never had growing up. She wasn't so certain she would find that with the present state of her broken family.

As far as Grace was concerned, Mercy could have them! She was still so angry over the secrecy and lies her *mamm* had concealed, that she wasn't sure if she would ever be able to look her *mamm* in the eye again. Her intention at the end of the week was to accept Seth's proposal and get married as soon as possible to avoid any further dealings with her family—a family she felt estranged from.

Squeezing herself into Mercy's *skinny jeans,* Grace couldn't help but wonder how long it would take her sister to throw in the towel and give up her identity in order to be able to wear her own clothes again. It would be worse for Mercy the first time a cold wind blew up the dress she would have to wear.

"Are you sure you can handle being cold in *mei* dresses for an entire week?"

Mercy laughed nervously. "It's too late to change my mind now. I already agreed, and I'm a woman of my word. I can handle anything for a few days. Just don't expect that I'm going to become Amish now that we are sisters!"

"No more than I would become an *Englischer* for you!"

"I suppose this is it. You remember how to work the microwave, yes?"

Grace nodded.

"I've stocked the fridge with plenty of food. Just promise me you won't burn down my apartment with my modern appliances!"

Grace laughed. "You don't have to worry about me using the stove. I don't even use the one at home! And I promise I will *try* my hardest not to burn down your apartment. But you also have to promise you won't get into a squabble with Lilly."

"What if she makes me mad?"

"You won't win any argument with her, so there isn't any point in trying, so I just walk away from her, and you will have to do the same."

Mercy grumbled under her breath, but she agreed reluctantly. "I guess this is it. If you want to change your mind, now is the time to do it."

Grace looked at herself in the mirror. She'd allowed Mercy to show her how to put on mascara, and she hadn't done such a bad job of it. Perhaps with a little practice, she would get better, but she likely wouldn't use it the rest of the week. She'd only put it on to appease her sister. She slipped into the red coat and pulled at the shortened length of her hair. She thought to herself that she would probably continue to pull her hair back once Mercy left, but for now it would stay down.

"I can't believe that I'm looking in the mirror and seeing us, but we are not ourselves. It's amazing how much we look alike."

"That's because we both look like our father," Mercy said. "You gonna be okay with meeting him?"

"*Jah.* I think it's the only way I'm going to come to terms with all of this, don't you think?"

"I suppose. But he's a selfish and greedy man. He's not going to be the sort of *father* you're used to. Just don't let him break your heart, Grace."

"It's a little too late for that, don't you think? He did all of that when he chose not to take care of *mei mamm* when he'd left her in a bad way."

It's funny that it had not occurred to Grace until then that her *mamm* had done the best she could in the situation she was in. She was older than her *mamm* had been when she'd had her, but yet she couldn't imagine bearing such a burden alone at such a young age. She suddenly felt sorry for her *mamm,* and had a new respect for her *daed* for stepping up and taking care of her and her *mamm* when it wasn't his responsibility to do so. It wasn't enough to cover the hurt Grace felt over the secrecy, but it was a start. Perhaps time would heal these wounds, but for now, she was happy for the extra time to think about her life.

As they exited the bathroom, her *daed's* buggy pulled up to the coffee shop. Mercy handed Grace the keys to her new temporary life, and then went out to meet her own.

CHAPTER 25

"*Mamm,* Grace just stuck her tongue out at me!" Lilly complained.

So you're a tattletale! Perhaps you need to learn a lesson, Mercy thought.

Walking over to the counter, she nudged Lilly out of the way and took the eggs. One-by-one, she cracked them into the porcelain bowl with one hand. Then she grabbed the fork and began to whip them up nice and fluffy, adding a little milk to make them richer. She tested the iron skillet by tapping her fingers on the hot surface, making certain the flame was not too high. Then, she poured in the mixture and began to scrape the sides to bring them to a nice fluffy scramble, all while her *mother* and *sister* stood aside and watched with mouths agape. While they finished cooking, Mercy took a few sheets of paper towels from the roll and placed them on a plate and lifted the crisp bacon from the other iron skillet. She turned off the flame and set the pan aside using a folded tea-towel. Then she reached into the cupboard and grabbed a large serving bowl and scooped the finished scrambled eggs into it.

Up until this time, Mercy had remained in the background and kept quiet as she could be. Even her ride home with Jacob had been silent. But now, after she'd had a fitful night of trying to sleep in Grace's uncomfortable bed and was forced to be up at this unnatural hour, she was becoming a little impatient with Lilly. Impatient enough to do exactly the opposite of what Grace had asked her to do.

No, Grace had actually begged her not to get into a squabble with Lilly, but now it was too late. It was on. It was to the point that Mercy had only been around the girl for less than a full day, and already she'd had enough of being picked on by her. It was time to put the girl in her place and take back Grace's life! She would either be very angry with Mercy when she returned, or she would be grateful for the change it brought on. Either way, Mercy would not be quiet even a moment longer.

"Do we have a cheese grater, *mamm?*" Mercy asked.

Lilly pointed to the cupboard next to the stove. "*Danki,*" she said with a perfect accent.

Mercy took the block of cheddar from the refrigerator and began to grate it over the scrambled eggs. Then she searched the pantry until she located a container of powdered sugar. After pulling the bran muffins from the oven, she grabbed a small bowl and put in a dab of butter and added a little cream, plus a few drops of vanilla, and whipped it with a fork. Then she added the powdered sugar, leaving it runny. Using the tea-towel to remove the muffins from the pan, she set them on a plate and drizzled the sugary mixture over the tops—all while the other two women in the kitchen watched in shock.

"Set the table so we can eat," she ordered Lilly.

The girl was too stunned to object and went about the task of setting the table. Their mother stepped outside the kitchen and clanged the dinner bell, and soon, her husband and son were inside ready for the morning meal that *Grace* had prepared.

Grace filled Mercy's bathtub with hot water and poured in bubbles. She'd never had a bubble bath before, but her sister had told her it was heavenly, so of course she had to try it.

"No girl should go her whole life without taking a bubble bath," Mercy had told her.

Grace intended on taking a leisurely morning bath and then she would watch more TV. Mercy had hundreds of channels, and Grace had found something interesting to watch until she'd finally gotten sleepy after midnight. She'd never had a reason to stay up that late—not even for a date with Seth. While all the other girls in the community would often stay out until the wee hours of the morning with their beaus, Grace never saw reason to stay out late with Seth. She wasn't so infatuated with him like all the other girls in the community were over their beaus.

In fact, she thought that Seth could be down-right boring sometimes, and she worried how things would be once they were married. Would they be bored with one another? They already didn't talk much when they got together. She'd often thought to herself that it was fortunate for her that Seth was so handsome, or she wouldn't be able to stand to be around him at all. It was shallow to think such a thing, she knew, but she'd often wondered the same thing of him. All he ever talked about was how pretty she was. They were certainly attracted to each other, there was no doubt about that. But was that all there was to it? Did they really love each other, or were they confusing physical attraction with love?

Grace slipped into the warmth of the tub, the water reaching up to her chin. Mercy had been right. A bubble bath was definitely something she could get used to. She closed her eyes and pondered her life a little more. She was relaxed now. Most of the tension from her decision seemed neutralized by the bubbles and hot water. Funny how such a simple thing could renew the mind so quickly.

When the water started to cool down, Grace pulled the plug and stepped out to dry off. That, she thought, was one luxury she would be sad to leave behind when she went back home.

Perhaps Seth would want to marry me enough to put in a big bathtub in our marital home, she thought with a giggle.

A large bathtub would not fix the troubles she faced in a marriage with Seth. She'd suddenly come to realize there wasn't anything that was going to make the relationship between them any stronger than it was—not even time like she'd originally thought.

Sadly, the best thing she could do for both of them would be to reject his proposal and hope her parents would let her get away with it. She'd been in denial about Seth for some time, but she now understood the only reason she'd considered his proposal in the first place was because of her parents' influence. That, and the fact that Simon Bontrager had left at the peak of their relationship. She'd cried for weeks, she'd missed him so much. If truth be told, she missed him even now.

What was she to do?

She supposed the *only* thing she could do would be to break things off with Seth, and she would take care of it immediately upon her return home.

Like ripping off a Band-Aid.

CHAPTER 26

Grace had just finished getting dressed when she heard a knock at Mercy's door. Panic filled her as she realized Mercy didn't go over what she should do if someone actually showed up at her door. She'd shown her how to use the peephole in the door if she heard a noise out in the hall, but anything beyond that she was on her own. She thought about ignoring it, but when she heard a key turning the lock, she picked up Mercy's phone intending to call 911, which Mercy also showed her how to do.

Suddenly the door pushed open and stopped abruptly against the chain on the door. Grace shook as she pushed the numbers on the phone and looked for the *send* button.

"Mercy, it's me—open the door!" an impatient male voice demanded.

"M-me, who?" Grace asked, her finger at the ready on the button to call for help.

"Mercy that isn't funny. I know you're mad at me, but don't pretend you don't know your own father's voice."

Grace let out the breath she'd been holding and walked to the door with wobbly legs. She'd feared such a meeting with the man, but Mercy had told her there was a possibility she's be able to meet him. Ready or not, she was about to meet her *real daed.*

What if he knows I'm not Mercy?

Grace shook off the negative thought and opened the door. Mercy had been right about one thing. She looked just like him—except that he was a man in his forties!

"Why aren't you ready to go?"

Grace looked at him blankly.

He looked at his watch. "It *is* Tuesday, and it *is* ten o'clock. We go to breakfast every week this same time, but yet I always have to wait for you to finish getting ready. I actually have to be back in the office before lunch today so I'm going to need you to hurry and get your coat on so we can go—unless you want to skip it this week."

"N-no—we can go. Just give me a minute to put my hair up."

"Your hair looks the same as it always does. Grab your coat, Pumpkin, and let's go!"

How could he say she looked the same as she always does? She guessed that he and Mercy were not so close that he wouldn't even know his own daughter if she was standing right in front of him.

It upset her a little that Mercy had neglected to warn her about her long-standing breakfast date with their father. What else had she neglected to tell her? Was there perhaps a boyfriend she'd forgotten to mention? She prayed not. Sitting through breakfast with her father was going to be painful enough. She couldn't imagine having to deal with a boyfriend she also didn't know.

Grace pushed her arms into Mercy's red coat and put on her gloves and scarf. She started to walk out the door when her father threw her the set of keys that hung by the door.

"Let's take your car," he said as he answered his cell phone.

"I can't drive," Grace squealed.

He pushed his face away from his phone.

"Mine just had a wash and I'd like to keep it clean for when I take my client out to the new building later, so we have to take yours."

"But I can't drive," Grace repeated.

He wasn't listening to her.

He was too busy listening to the person on the other end of his phone.

Grace began to shake and pray that the man meant that he would do the driving. She had barely driven a buggy because her own father didn't allow her to go much farther than two farms down with it. He'd certainly never allowed her to drive it into town, claiming he worried she would get into an accident.

"Or we could go to the diner across the street," Grace suggested nervously.

"Why would we go to that dive? We always go to Mirabella's."

Why did I agree to go? Now I'm going to have to drive and I can't drive, and I don't have a driver's license, and he thinks I'm Mercy. Ach what am I going to do?

She was practically hysterical.

She stared at the man who was a complete stranger to her. Was he really that oblivious to his own daughter that he didn't realize she was not Mercy? How was she going to handle driving Mercy's car when she couldn't even handle the man right in front of her.

Mercy was right about one thing.

Their father was selfish.

He motioned for her to follow him out of the apartment while he nodded and agreed with whoever he was talking to on his phone. Not knowing what to do, she followed him, praying he would drive. She tried to hand him the keys but he shook his head at her as he talked to the person on his phone.

Think, she commanded herself. *What should I do? I'm gonna have to tell him I'm not his daughter. Well, I am, but not the one he thinks I am!*

She pushed the keys toward him again as they approached Mercy's car. Mercy had taken her for a ride in it, but had not offered to let her drive it. She'd warned her not to burn down her apartment. How would she feel if Grace put a dent in her car?

Her father put his hand over the receiver.

"You need to drive," he said sternly. "Can't you see I'm on the phone?"

He opened the passenger side door and sat down, talking away on the phone. Grace reluctantly slipped into the driver's side praying, and feeling like she was going to pass out from fear. She sat there shaking until her father hung up his phone and turned to her.

"Start the car, Mercy, and let's go, or we won't have time to eat before my meeting."

She put her shaky hands on the steering wheel to brace herself.

"I can’t drive," she whispered.

"What do you mean you can’t drive? Mercy, what is wrong with you this morning?"

"I can’t drive because I’m not Mercy," she whispered, tears streaming down her cheeks. "I’m Grace!"

CHAPTER 27

"Grace," Lilly said as she poked her head inside her sister's bedroom door. "Seth is here."

Mercy ignored the girl and went about folding the extra quilt at the end of the bed. She was exhausted from working with Jonah most of the day, but she had to admit that Grace had been right about him; he was fun to hang out with. He had even taken her down to the creek and they'd found a new rock for his collection. Right now, all she wanted to do was rest for a little while until dinner time. She didn't want to be bothered with Seth, and least of all, Lilly.

"You shouldn't keep him waiting," Lilly warned. "Most of the girls in the community want Seth, and he'll find someone else if you keep him waiting."

Mercy smirked at her. "I'm not worried about that."

"Well, you should be!"

Mercy glared at her. "And I think you should mind your own business."

Mercy grabbed a fashion magazine from under the bed and watched Lilly's eyes bulge out of her head as she flipped through the pages.

"I don't know what has gotten into you, Grace. I'm glad you felt the need to show off the new cooking tricks *Aenti* Sadie obviously taught you while you stayed with her, but nothing has changed around here. Just because we don't really have the same *daed,* doesn't mean you can get away with doing whatever you want to now. You have an obligation to Seth, and if you don't want him, I'll marry him. You should start taking your relationship with him seriously—especially now that you aren't exactly part of this *familye* anymore."

Mercy slammed the magazine down and stood up abruptly, causing Lilly to jump.

"What makes you think I'm not a part of this *familye* now? Because we don't share the same *daed?* The way I see it, I'm more a part than you are since *daed* chose to raise me when he didn't have to. With *you* he had no choice!"

Lilly ran screaming from the room, and came back moments later with her *mamm,* pointing out the magazine Mercy was looking at, and vying for her sister to be reprimanded for viewing reading material that wasn't approved by the Bishop.

When Lilly left the room, her *mother* simply told her to keep the magazine out of sight, and to stop aggravating Lilly. She smiled knowingly at Mercy, and she almost thought the woman knew she wasn't Grace, but she figured it was best to keep quiet about that for now. She hadn't even mentioned Seth, who was still waiting for *Grace*.

Curiosity getting the better of her, Mercy decided to go and meet Seth. If Grace wasn't going to have enough guts to break it off with Seth, she would do it for her. She went to the stairway and began her decent when her gaze locked on his.

Why is Grace going to break up with him?

He's so gorgeous!

Mercy couldn't take her eyes off him. All six feet of him was trim and muscular. His chiseled jaw held fast to a dimpled smile, which she returned to him. His wavy hair was thick and sun-kissed like a surfer's hair.

Yes, Seth was certainly *eye-candy.*

Mercy shook herself from her thoughts, trying desperately to remember that he was still her sister's boyfriend until the girl broke up with him.

She *was* going to break up with him.

And she was going to do it as soon as she returned home, as a matter of fact.

Mercy couldn't wait that long. She felt an irresistible urge to kiss Seth, and she wanted to kiss him *now*.

But she wouldn't. She shouldn't.

It wouldn't be right, would it?

He was practically a free man.

Only a technicality made him not free.

Mercy looped her arm in Seth's and led him out the door. "Take me for a buggy ride," she said with a smile.

"I brought the sleigh," he said with a sultry baritone that Mercy found irresistible. "We've never taken a sleigh ride, and I thought it would be special."

He smiled and took her hand in his, leading her to his sleigh. Once she was settled, he placed a lap-quilt around her and set his horses in motion. The jingling of the bells on their harnesses made Mercy think of Christmas. She felt like she was in the middle of a fairytale. With a handsome prince sitting very close to her, and the romance of the sleigh ride, she couldn't ask for a more perfect evening with a more perfect man.

Except he thinks he's with Grace, Mercy reminded herself. *But maybe I should fix that.*

Did she dare tell him who she was?

Seth moved in closer to her and put his arm around her.

"You seem different," he said to her. "Like a whole different person. I like the change in you."

He knows! This is my chance.

"Probably because I *am* a different person," she admitted.

"I agree. I think that vacation you took made you into a whole new person. I like the new you."

Mercy couldn't take it anymore.

She had to kiss him or she was going to burst at the seams.

He stopped the sleigh under the stars at the edge of the creek, the moonlight illuminating his handsome face. She closed the space between them and brought her face forward, his full lips her target. His arms went around her and his lips nearly touched hers. She was so close she could feel his warm breath on her cheek. But he suddenly pulled away from her.

"I thought you said you wanted to wait until we got married," he said nervously.

"To kiss you?" Mercy asked louder than she'd intended.

"*Jah,* I agreed not to kiss you or anything else until after the wedding. I'm surprised you let me hold your hand."

If Grace didn't even want to kiss him, there is no way she loves him!

Mercy reached back and pulled her hair loose from the *kapp* and the pins that bound it, while Seth watched her with desire in his eyes.

"You made that deal with Grace," she said with a smile. "I'm Mercy, and I want you to kiss me!"

"If you say so!"

Seth cupped his hands around Mercy's face and pulled her to him until her lips met his. His kiss was sweet like peppermint and hot cocoa, and Mercy deepened the kiss, passion driving her.

She could easily fall in love with Seth!

CHAPTER 28

Mercy readied herself for her date with Seth. She had never met a man so gentle and caring in her life. She was already head-over-heels in love with him, and she was certain he felt the same way about her. She'd steered away from the subject of Grace the entire week, as Mercy had not wanted to remind him that he still had unfinished business with her. Really it was only a formality, and as soon as Grace returned tomorrow, her sister would officially break it off with him, then she and Seth would be free to have a relationship that didn't fill Mercy with guilt and worry.

Her only serious worry was that Grace would change her mind and want to marry Seth after all.

When she'd talked to Grace last night, all she could talk about was to go on and on about how their dad was teaching her to drive. He'd taught Mercy to drive, and he had not been a patient teacher. She hoped for Grace's sake that he was being more patient with her. Mercy was so infatuated with Seth that she didn't care that Grace had been driving her new convertible. But if it all worked out between her and Seth, Mercy would no longer have a need for the car, and the thought of it didn't bother her in the least.

She'd neglected to mention to Grace that she was seeing Seth, but she'd been quite secretive since she'd entered Grace's life, right down to hiding her cell phone in the barn overnight to charge, using the only electrical outlet that they had.

Grace's dad used the electricity for his business, but he would never allow the use of a phone in his home since it was against the rules of the Ordnung. Mercy had used the single outlet after Grace had told her it existed. Without Grace's help, she'd have never found it, as it was well-hidden. And seeing that the house itself was devoid of electricity, Mercy would have never thought to look in the barn for such a thing—

especially since the electrical wires were all buried underground.

One last look in her compact mirror, and Mercy felt she was ready for her date. She was getting used to not wearing makeup, and actually liked the freedom from it.

She heard Seth's sleigh pull into the yard and she peeked out her window to be sure. She ran down the stairs, delight filling her.

Jacob met up with her on the front porch.

"I'm pleased to see you've changed your mind about Seth. He'll make a fine husband."

"*Jah,* he will," Mercy said with a smile as she ran out to the dark driveway to meet her *boyfriend.*

His waiting arms felt good as she melted into him. "I missed you today, Sweet-pea," he said in her ear.

It sent shivers right through her, and his new nick-name for her was the cutest thing she'd ever heard. He'd told her she smelled like the wild flowers that grew along the meadow near his family farm, and so he'd started calling her Sweet-pea from that first date they'd had.

Now, as she felt his strong arms around her, she felt assured that nothing could break the bond between them. "Let's get you settled in and get a lap-quilt around you so we can enjoy this light snow a little better."

Once again, Mercy snuggled up against Seth, his strong arms making her feel safe. She couldn't imagine ever wanting to be anywhere else but in his arms.

Before long, they reached Seth's farm and he pulled the sleigh into a secluded area in front of a little house.

"Here we are, Sweet-pea. I'll have you warmed up in just a few minutes."

She pushed out pouty lips. "My lips are cold too!"

He began kissing her, pulling her closer than he'd held her before. "I love you, Sweet-pea," he said between kisses. "I wish you'd marry me."

"Of course I'll marry you!" she said deepening his kiss.

"You have made me the happiest *mann*!"

He jumped up from the seat of the sleigh and offered his hand to assist her out. "Come inside so I can show you where we will live. I'll build us a fire so you can warm up."

Mercy followed Seth into the *dawdi haus,* unable to contain her excitement.

Seth showed Mercy around the *dawdi haus*, avoiding the bedroom, where he was certain he'd left some personal laundry on the floor. Then he asked her if she would mind making some hot cocoa for the two of them while he put away his horses in the barn.

He'd already started a fire, and it was beginning to burn the logs he'd put in.

Mercy looked around the kitchen that would soon be hers. It was primitive compared to the kitchen in her apartment, but none of that mattered to her. She was going to be married to a beautiful, kind man, and she couldn't be happier. She made fast work of getting the hot cocoa heated on the gas stove, knowing it wouldn't take long for her betrothed to put away the horses.

Her betrothed.

She could not think of anything else. She giggled at the thought of how her father was going to react when she told him she was engaged to be married to an Amish man. She wondered what Seth would want to do with the building she owned. She assumed they would rent out her apartment and it would be a nice income for them.

They had a lot to sort out before they got married, and they didn't have much time.

Grace would certainly have to show her how to do the things she needed to know in order to be a good Amish wife. That is, once she got over the shock of Mercy's relationship with Seth. She hoped it would not be awkward between her and Grace where Seth was concerned, but she didn't foresee any problems. She was certain Grace would be happy for her. Mercy couldn't wait to share her feelings with her sister, but she would wait until Grace was home, and all ties were severed between her and Seth.

When Seth entered in through the kitchen door, his arms were full of firewood, and snow blew in. Mercy rushed to close the door for him so he could drop the freshly-chopped wedges near the hearth. As she filled the porcelain cups with hot cocoa, she could hear Seth in the other room putting more wood on the fire. She brought the cups in and sat down on the sofa while he adjusted the logs in the fire so they would burn brighter.

When he was satisfied with the blaze he'd created, he took off his coat and picked up the quilt at the end of the sofa, then wrapped it around his and Mercy's shoulders. She handed him his cup of cocoa, and he sipped the hot liquid slowly at first, wrapping his hands around the mug to warm them. Then he gulped the rest of it down within a minute. Taking Mercy's cup, he set them both down in front of him without a word.

"We have a lot to talk about," Mercy said.

"*Jah,* we do," he agreed. "But right now, all I want to do is kiss my Sweet-pea and celebrate that you said yes to my proposal."

Seth closed the space between them, placing kisses on her neck and cheeks, and finally on her lips. She leaned into him, her hands probing the contours of his chest.

"I'm so happy we will be married soon. I love you, Sweet-pea."

"I love you too," she said, deepening the kiss, and allowing Seth's passion for her to take over.

If she had her way, they'd be married already.

CHAPTER 29

Mercy woke up next to Seth, who had one arm and one leg dangling off the sofa.

Panic consumed her, tears welling up in her throat.

What had they done?

They'd allowed their passion for one another to cloud their judgment. All her life, Mercy had promised herself she would not repeat her mother's mistakes, having learned how she'd come to be in this world. But yet here she was, and she'd made the same mistake her mother had.

Daylight barely shone through the sheer curtains over the large window in the sitting room where they'd fallen asleep.

Mercy had heard the jokes from other girls about the *walk of shame* the morning after such an act, and she never thought in a million years she would be participating in such a vile practice. She certainly felt shame for the mistake she'd made in judgment; that she was certain of. But now she would have to face Seth—unless she could find her…

Where is my dress?

Mercy tried to slip out from around Seth's dead weight, but he was on her hair, and, oh, the quilt was wrapped around their legs and under her. If she tried to crawl free from her entanglement with Seth, she'd surely roll him to the floor.

That would not be good.

Feeling mortified, she knew there was nothing to do but wait until he shifted his position or woke up.

For a moment, she watched him sleep. He was so beautiful, and she truly loved him, but they had taken things too far, too soon. She'd made a promise to herself, and now she'd broken it.

How was she going to escape this with her dignity intact? It was definitely too late for that. There was no amount of wishing on her part that could turn back the hands of time and force her to be more responsible, or to have more respect for herself than this. Would Seth still respect her? Or would he look at her differently now?

But we're getting married in just a few weeks, she tried to reason with herself.

That didn't work.

Regret still consumed her. Not regret for loving Seth, but for not waiting for that special night.

Her wedding night.

Seth woke up and stared at her blankly as he ran a hand through his messy hair until it registered where he was, and with whom.

"Oh no! I'm so sorry. We should have waited until..."

He didn't finish the sentence.

There was no point when they both knew what he was going to say.

"Pull yourself together and I'll have you home before morning chores," he said abruptly as he wiped the sleep from his eyes.

He rose from the sofa and dressed quickly in the same clothes that had been scattered across the floor in the heat of passion. He picked up the dress he'd helped her out of last night, pausing to think of the transgression he'd committed against her. He handed her the dress without looking her in the eye. He couldn't because he was too embarrassed.

He knew his first mistake was in bringing her to his home and expecting he could easily control his emotions enough to honor her the way he should have. She was not yet his, but he'd taken from her, and now he would have to make it right.

Guilt filled Seth as he went out to the barn to hitch the horses to the buggy. He had to get her out of the *dawdi haus* and back home before either of their families ventured out for the day. If she was to be seen, it could ruin her reputation and cause the Bishop to question their commitment to one another and to the rules of the Ordnung. They would surely be reprimanded far beyond the regret he felt now.

Seth pulled the buggy up to the back side of the *dawdi haus*. Mercy exited the back door slowly, making certain no one was around to witness her escape from shame. She couldn't even look Seth in the eye. He didn't say one word to her as he assisted her into the buggy.

Though she sat only inches from him, they seemed miles apart in spirit. They rode in silence the entire ride home, making it more awkward than it had to be. But what was there to say? Perhaps later, when they'd both had time to sort out what had happened they would be able to talk about it. It needed to be talked about so it didn't happen again until they were married.

Would they still be married?

CHAPTER 30

Grace parked Mercy's car back into the wooded area about a quarter mile away from Seth's house. She fumbled with her *kapp,* making certain everything was in place for her talk with him. She wasn't certain she would ever let him know that she'd been living among the *Englisch* for the past two weeks. It wasn't anyone's business but hers and Mercy's, and neither of them would ever tell.

After wearing pants for the past week, she'd forgotten how cold it could be when the wind and snow blew up her dress. Pulling the bottom hem closer to her legs, she hoped to prevent the wind from cutting into her skin. She'd neglected to keep a pair of her thick stockings aside when she'd held onto her *going home* clothes. Mercy had taken everything else with her back to Grace's house. So now, here she was walking down the snowy road, regretting not parking the car a little closer. Honestly, with the trees bare, she couldn't get any closer without the risk of being seen, and so she walked until she reached his farm.

Grace was determined to get her talk with Seth over as quickly as possible. She'd put him off for too long, and she could not return home until she'd told him what she needed to say. What she should have said a long time ago.

As she approached the farm, she could see Seth outside the barn, fixing the latch on the door.

He barely looked up at her, but flashed her a shy smile nonetheless.

"Didn't expect to see you here now, but I'm glad to see you," he said as he approached her awkwardly. "Did you get through your morning chores already?"

He bent to kiss her and she pushed him away.

"What are you doing? You think I want to kiss you now?" Grace asked angrily.

What had gotten into him while she was gone? Did he think her absence from him would make their bond stronger? It had done the opposite for her, and she needed to tell him quickly before he got any further notions in his head about the two of them.

"*Jah,* I did think you would want to kiss me—after…"

"I don't ever want to kiss you," she rudely interrupted him. "In fact, I don't want to see you anymore either. I'm not going to marry you, and there is no future for us. I should not have led you on, and I'm sorry for that, but I will be leaving the community for a while, and I don't know when I'll be back or if I will."

She hadn't meant to blurt it all out so haphazardly, but his attempt at kissing her had put her into shock.

She didn't share with him that she was going to pursue a future with Simon. It was hard enough telling him what she knew she had to. She wouldn't hurt him further by flaunting her new relationship with Simon in his face.

"Why are you doing this? I love you, and I thought you loved me."

He was practically in tears, and Grace felt sorry for him.

"I don't love you, and I'm sorry if I did anything that made you think otherwise. I've made up my mind. Please respect my decision, and let it go. Let *me* go."

Seth turned his back to her. He couldn't say a word to her without breaking down. What had changed since he'd dropped her off only a short time ago? Did she regret what had happened between them? They'd certainly made a mistake in judgment, but he'd had time to think about things since he'd dropped her off, and he intended to honor her by marrying her—immediately, if possible. It was obvious to him that she had no desire to be his Sweet-pea. No desire to marry him the way he'd thought she did, and so he would have to let her go no matter how much it hurt. He would not bind her to him if she wasn't willing to marry him.

He could not understand why she had agreed to marry him if she was now ending it between them. Had she changed her mind, or had she had no intention of marrying him to begin with? But if that was the case, why would she have lied to him? This was not how it was supposed to be, but now he was powerless to stop it.

"I'm sorry," she said quietly.

Grace walked away, tears filling her eyes. She had not meant to hurt him, but it was obvious she had. Regret filled her over the amount of time she'd let her own selfish wants keep her bound to him when she'd needed to let him go much sooner for his sake.

She walked back down the road toward Mercy's car. She was supposed to be meeting her in a few minutes at the abandoned Bontrager farm, but she was going to be a little late.

Grace pulled Mercy's car into the curved driveway of Simon Bontrager's abandoned farm. She'd seen him a couple of times this past week while she'd stayed at Mercy's apartment, after accidentally bumping into him at the coffee shop. It was still too soon to know if anything would come of their *dates,* but she intended to return to the city to pursue Simon.

Though he'd liked her *new look,* she intended to go back to her old ways. It was what she was comfortable with. It was familiar, and she needed all the familiarity she could find right now. She had decided that for now, she would not become a part of the community, but she would continue to live as though she was—observing the customs without becoming a member of the church through baptism just yet.

She couldn't wait to share her decisions with Mercy, but that could wait until later when her mood improved. She was still so shaken up from the talk with Seth that she was not in the right frame of mind to be sharing good news just yet. For now, she would exchange the keys and their lives with Mercy, and they could talk in a few days when Grace returned to the city.

When she parked the car, she could see that Mercy was waiting for her on the porch swing.

Just keep the conversation to familye-related topics, Grace told herself before exiting Mercy's car.

Mercy stood up to greet her with downcast eyes.

She's really playing the part, isn't she?

What she didn't realize was that Mercy was too ashamed to look her in the eye.

"I see that our father taught you well. But you do know that you aren't supposed to be driving without a licensed driver beside you until you get your own license, don't you?"

Grace shook her head and shrugged her shoulders.

"It's a *gut* thing I was careful then," she said nervously.

Mercy sat back down on the porch swing and Grace joined her. They sat silent for what seemed a short lifetime before Grace couldn't take it anymore.

"You're being way too quiet, Mercy. What happened while I was gone? Did you get into a fight with Lilly after I asked you not to?"

Mercy had forgotten about that! That would be an easy story to tell Grace compared to telling her what had happened between her and Seth.

She didn't want to share her news about Seth just yet—especially after what had happened between them. She didn't want Grace knowing they'd taken things too far. As an Amish woman, she didn't think Grace would understand, and would make her feel more shame than she already did. She would wait a few days until she was able to absorb the enormity of the situation herself. She hadn't quite had time to process it, but she prayed that Seth would agree to marry her immediately to avoid another mistake that could cost him his status in the community, or worse, to cause him to change his opinion of her.

Mercy nodded after another minute of silence. "I did fight with her a couple of times, but it's not as bad as you'd think. That girl is what we *Englischers* would call a *mean-girl.* But I think you'll see that Lilly's going to leave you alone from now on."

"What did you do?"

"I cooked an awesome breakfast right in front of her and your mother. You should have seen the look on her face when she saw *you* making breakfast like a five-star chef."

Grace laughed at the thought of Lilly's anguish, and Mercy joined her.

"I suppose I have to go home now," Grace said. "*Danki* for taking my place here for the last week so I could have more time to think about my life—*and* for putting Lilly in her place."

"I'm glad I came here, Grace. I wouldn't trade my experiences here for anything. It's changed my life."

"It seems to have done you some *gut,* and I'm happy for you. I'll be coming to visit you in a couple of days."

"You're coming back to the city? Why?"

Grace winced at the question. "Let's just say I have some unfinished business there. How about we talk about it then? Right now, I need to get home and have a long talk with *mei mamm* and *daed.*"

Mercy was relieved Grace didn't want to talk now. All she could think about was Seth, and she wasn't up to talking about that yet either.

"That sounds like a good idea. We'll have a good long talk when you come for a visit," Mercy agreed.

Grace stood up and gave Mercy a long hug. She had missed her sister while she was away, but they would have plenty of time next week to tell each other everything.

CHAPTER 31

Mercy hopped in her car and waved to Grace as she drove away. She decided she would stop by and see Seth before she drove back to the city. They needed to talk, and if he wasn't too busy, she hoped he would take the time to tell her what she needed to hear right now—that everything was going to be alright, and they could get married immediately.

Deciding it was best that his family not see her as an *Englischer* just yet—or at least until she knew for sure that he'd shared it with them, she would park her car down the road a ways, and walk to his farm. She found a little inlet in a wooded area and parked there.

Mercy walked up the long driveway where she found Seth outside the barn replacing the rusty handles. When he saw her approach, he seemingly ignored her and continued with his task. She stood there for a minute waiting for him to finish, thinking that he would stop what he was doing and talk to her but he didn't.

"Seth," she finally said.

He hesitated.

Why was she torturing him like this? Hadn't she hurt him enough less than an hour ago when she'd broken up with him?

"What are you doing back here so soon? I thought you were leaving town."

How did he know about that? If she didn't know him better, she'd think he was irritated with her.

"Are you upset because I'm leaving?"

"Are you serious? That's only part of it. Why did you come back here? What do you want?"

"I was hoping we could talk a little bit."

"What is there left to talk about? Are you here to clear your conscience?"

"No!"

"I don't think there's anything left to be said. I know I have nothing more to say to you," he said as he turned his backside toward her. "I think you should leave."

Mercy felt like he'd punched her in her gut.

She couldn't breathe.

Tears welled up in her throat, choking her.

Her tears quickly turned to sobs as she doubled over, covering her mouth with her hand.

Forced breaths seeped through the fingers that clamped over her mouth as she tried to squelch her sobs. Why was he rejecting her now? Had he only said he loved her and asked her to marry him because he planned to take advantage of her?

Seth turned around abruptly. "Why are you crying? You got what you wanted from me. Now you can leave."

"You think all I wanted was to sleep with you?" she asked, sobs catching in her throat.

"That's the way it looks. So I suppose we *both* got what we wanted."

He didn't mean it, but he couldn't let her know how much she'd hurt him. He wanted to go to her and hold her close, promising her everything would work out, but she'd said her peace to him earlier, and he would not hear another word from her. He'd been weak earlier when she'd broken up with him and had shown her his emotions.

He wouldn't make that mistake again.

Mercy's wobbly legs turned her around and shuffled her toward the road. She could barely see around the tears that wouldn't stop, and her ragged breaths mixed with uncontrollable sobs.

How could she have fallen for the oldest trick in the book? Had he really used a proposal of marriage to have his way with her? She would have never thought he was the type of man to do such a horrible thing, but his rejection of her was evident he was.

Now she'd soiled her reputation over an empty promise, and she supposed she was no longer worthy of marriage to him. What had changed? Had he had time to think, and now regretted being with her? They were from two different worlds.

What had she been thinking?

She would never trust another man as long as she lived. As far as she was concerned, they were all liars who would say anything to get what they wanted.

What was she to do now?

She'd turned out just like her mother.

She'd made the same mistake without even trying.

Would she now suffer the same fate?

CHAPTER 32

Grace walked in the back door of her family home just as Lilly was walking out.

Lilly did a double-take, staring at Grace.

"Didn't you have your blue dress on this morning?"

Grace glared at the nosy girl. "I think you're seeing things!"

Lilly stuck her tongue out and left the house without a comeback. Perhaps Mercy had done well to put the rude girl in her place after all. Grace could get used to having the upper hand over her younger sister for a change. She'd missed her sister, but Lilly didn't need to know that because for all she knew, Mercy had done a good enough job of fooling her while she was gone.

She found her *mamm* in the front room stoking the fire, her *daed* in his chair taking his usual thirty-minute nap following the afternoon meal. She was relieved they were both in the same place so she could get her talk over with as quickly and painlessly as possible.

She crossed the room and rested her head on her *mamm's* shoulder, which surprised the woman.

"What's this all about, Grace? I just talked to you an hour ago." The woman felt Grace's forehead with the back of her hand. "Are you feeling alright?"

"I'm fine, *mamm,* but I would like to talk to you and *daed* for a minute."

Her *mamm* put a hand on her husband's foot, causing him to open his eyes.

"What's on your mind, Grace?" her *daed* asked.

She twisted her hands nervously, trying her best to choose her words wisely. "I did a lot of thinking while I was staying with *Aenti* Sadie. I went through a lot of different feelings and experienced some up and down emotions about my discovery a couple of weeks ago. The fact that it caused you to share something so personal with me really means a lot to me.

I'll admit I felt anger and confusion over the situation at first, but I think you both handled it very well in the end. I'm a few years older than you were when this changed your life, and I know I would not have been able to handle it at all. I may not understand the whole thing, but I'm grateful for *Grossmammi* Ellie for doing the right thing and helping you to make the right decision for my life. And I'm grateful to you *Daed,* for raising me as your own *dochder* when you could have walked away just as easily as *mei* real *daed.*"

Jacob looked at her, his eyes glistening with emotion.

"That first time I held you, that was when you became *mei dochder.*"

Grace wiped a tear from her cheek. "You have been a very *gut daed* to me, and I'm thankful for that. You were certainly better than *mei* real *daed*, and I'm glad you raised me instead of him. He's not a kind man, and certainly not responsible."

"How do you know about him?" her *mamm* asked.

"Because I met him when I was in the city. I didn't go looking for him. He just happened to run into me."

Her parents looked at each other, and then back to her.

"I know it must have hurt you a great deal when he left you, *mamm,*" Grace continued. "But I'm glad he did because otherwise I would not have been raised by the best *daed* a girl could ever ask for. I appreciate the way you raised me—with *gut* strong morals and just enough love not to spoil me."

She turned again to her *mamm.* "It must have taken a lot of courage to raise me when you were both so young, but I'm glad you both chose to do the right thing for me. I couldn't have picked two better parents if *Gott* had given me the choice, but I'm glad He helped to make that choice. It's been a real blessing being a part of this *familye.*"

Her parents held out their arms to hug her and she went to them. She loved them both dearly, and she'd meant every word she'd said to them.

"Since I'm old enough to be out on my own, I need to stay for a little while longer with *Aenti* Sadie. She's getting on in years, and I want to help her any way I can. Besides, I have some unfinished business to pursue in the city, and I'd like the freedom to do that."

Her parents looked at each other again, nodded to each other, and then to Grace.

"I'll drive you whenever you're ready," her *daed* said, "And you can send word through the shared telephone in the center of the community when you want to return home."

Grace let out a sigh of relief. "*Danki* for being so understanding."

Just then Jonah came barreling into the room and dragged her into the kitchen, pulling her aside to hug her and whisper in her ear. "I missed you, Grace. But where did that other girl go?"

Her heart gave a jumpstart at his comment.

"What girl?" she asked cautiously.

"The one that looks like you. The one that stayed with us. She was nice. She helped me find a really *gut* rock."

Grace smiled at her inquisitive little brother.

"How did you know…?"

"That it wasn't you?" he interrupted.

Grace nodded curiously.

"I spend the most time with you. Did you think I wouldn't know it wasn't you? Did you think I wouldn't know *mei* own *schweschder?*"

"I'd hoped no one would know. You didn't tell *mamm* or *daed,* did you?"

"Of course not! I ain't a snitch."

"I'm glad you liked her. She's my *schweschder,* and her name is Mercy."

"Is she going to come back? She promised me she'd help me dig one of those blue rocks out of the bottom of the creek."

Grace put her arm around his shoulder.

"I'm not sure if she'll be back, but I'd be happy to help you get one of the blue rocks. I've had my eye on those for a while too. They're nice."

Grace wished she could answer Jonah's question, but she could no more do that than she could break the news to him that she, herself, was about to leave, and she had no idea when or if she would return.

Grace had come to realize that she liked her *Englisch* side almost as much as her Amish side, but she needed to see how it would affect the people most dear to her.

Now that she'd come to terms with the past, and had found out who she was, she was ready to discover what that meant for her future.

PART THREE: AMISH MERCY

CHAPTER 33

Grace pressed her ear to Mercy's door.

She pounded on it again impatiently. "Open this door! I can hear you crying, so I know you're in there."

"Go away!" Mercy finally hollered between sobs from the other side of the door.

At least she's answering me now, but I still have to get her to open the door.

Grace pounded on the door for the umpteenth time. "I've knocked on your door every day for the past week and you won't answer, and I know that you've been home because your car has not left the parking garage. I'm not leaving here until you open this door and tell me what's wrong."

The door swung open suddenly, and Mercy stood there, her blonde hair a ratty mess, her blue eyes blood-shot and red-rimmed against swollen, puffy lids.

She looked at Grace, anger and pain clouding her eyes. "Go back to your perfect life, Grace, and leave me alone!"

Mercy attempted to shut her out, but Grace slid her foot in between the frame and the solid wood door.

"What makes you think my life is so perfect?"

"Because it's not mine," Mercy sobbed.

Her shoulders shook as she ran into her apartment, leaving Grace at the door. Heaving herself onto her deep, leather sofa, Mercy muffled her uncontrollable sobs into the pillows.

Grace let herself into the apartment and closed the door. She went to her sister and sat beside her, rubbing her back lightly.

"We saw each other only two weeks ago, and you were in the best of spirits. What happened?"

"Men!" Mercy grumbled, sobbing even harder.

Well, now we're getting somewhere.

Not a subject Grace was experienced in, but she'd just had to break up with Seth, and that was not a pretty situation. She knew men could often be less mature than women at times, and he certainly hadn't let her down that day.

"What about them?" Grace asked, unsure if she wanted to hear the response.

"Go away, Grace," Mercy warned again. "You wouldn't understand."

"Try me!" she dared her sister.

Mercy sobbed harder. "I don't want to talk about this. Men are pigs, and you would be doing yourself a favor if you'd stay away from all of them. I know I will for the rest of my life."

Grace was a little confused. She didn't even know Mercy was dating anyone, much less, to have time to develop this kind of heartache from a relationship.

"*Pigs?*" Grace asked curiously.

Mercy lifted her tear-stained face from the depth of the pillows. "They are all jerks! They take what they want from you and toss you aside like you don't matter to them!"

Grace was almost afraid to ask. "Did a man do this to you?"

Wiping her runny nose, Mercy sobbed even harder, throwing herself back onto the pillows.

"It can't be *that* bad, can it?"

"Grace, what are you doing here?" Mercy asked through gritted teeth.

"*Ach,* I came straight from the bus station. You told me I could stay with you while I'm in the city, remember? But since you haven't answered your door for the past week I had to stay with *mei aenti.*"

Mercy raised her head from the pillows again, her expression blank. "I changed my mind. Go back home where you belong."

"My place is here with you if you need me," Grace offered.

"Go away, Grace!" Mercy said, raising her voice in anger. "I don't need *you.* I don't need *anyone!"*

Mercy unexpectedly jumped up from the sofa, holding her stomach, and ran to the bathroom, Grace on her heels. She collapsed over the toilet, the contents of her stomach heaving her whole body. Grace knelt down behind her and pulled her wayward hair out of the way with one hand and rubbed her back with the other.

"You need to calm down, dear *schweschder.* You're making yourself sick with all of this."

Mercy lifted her head up from the bowl and looked at Grace, her cheeks pink and her skin pale.

"I didn't make myself sick—he..."

She didn't finish her sentence before her head was back in the bowl for round two.

Grace rubbed her back and handed Mercy a tissue to wipe her mouth. Helping her to her feet, she managed to get her wobbly-legged sister back to the sofa. Once she was comfortable, she tucked a throw blanket around her to keep her warm.

She crossed to the fireplace and stoked the fire, piling another log onto it. Soon, the room filled with the crackling sound of wood burning, and Grace was grateful that for now, at least, Mercy's sobs had diminished.

CHAPTER 34

No sooner did Grace think Mercy had worn herself out and dozed off than she began to shake with fresh sobs. Grace went into the kitchen and put on the kettle for tea. She could do that much for her sister. She didn't know what else to do; she didn't know how to react. She loved Mercy, and couldn't bear to see her hurting so much, but what could she do when the girl would not trust her with her troubles?

Grace stood at the stove feeling helpless to comfort Mercy. Whispering a short prayer, she knew that was all she could do for her sister besides being there for her. She was determined to stay and care for her, despite Mercy's quarrelsome attitude toward her. Though she didn't understand how Mercy could have had such a dramatic change in her life in the span of only two weeks since she'd last seen her, she understood that it had to be painful in order for her to react the way she was.

Grace shrugged off her worries for the moment, as she focused on making tea without setting her sister's kitchen on fire. The last thing she wanted was to upset Mercy more than she already was. When the tea kettle began to whistle, she turned off the flame beneath it and dropped a tea bag into the fancy china cup, and then poured the steaming water over it. She bounced the tea bag mindlessly a few times, struggling to remember anything Mercy might have said to her that might provide a clue as to her present woes.

The only man Mercy had ever mentioned was the lawyer who rented the ground floor of her building. The way she'd casually spoken of him left no reason for Grace to think he was the one who'd broken her heart. But her sister had not mentioned even dating anyone, let alone, being in love. She couldn't imagine loving someone that early in the relationship that she could become this upset over an obvious *breakup*.

Taking the tea into the living room, she set it on the coffee table in front of Mercy, and watched as the girl picked up the cup in a curious fashion. With her pinkie finger extended outward, she held the delicate, narrow handle with two fingers as she lifted it to her lips. Grace thought it was a bit dramatic for drinking tea, but Mercy was quite the dramatic person.

Sitting down on the sofa at Mercy's feet, Grace found it difficult to maintain a quiet and humble manner as she reflected on just how different the two of them really were. Looking alike was not the same as *being* alike. They were as opposite as two sisters could be—more than even her and Lilly.

"I wish you would tell me what was wrong," Grace begged. "I'm your sister. You can tell me anything."

Mercy sat up and smirked at Grace. "I can't tell you *anything.* I'm in enough pain, and I'm not up for being judged by you and your perfectly pure life."

"My life is not so perfect. Do you forget that we are cut from the same cloth?"

“That doesn’t mean you will understand what I’m going through,” Mercy sobbed harder. “I’d be willing to bet everything I have that you’ve *never* been through what I just went through.”

Grace sighed. “Is it really that bad?”

Mercy looked up at her, tears pooling in her puffy eyes. “It’s so horrible I’m not even sure I believe it myself!”

“What could possibly be that terrible?”

“Falling in love!” Mercy said sarcastically.

“*Ach,* falling in love is not terrible,” Grace debated.

“It is when he doesn’t love you back! I will never let myself fall in love again!” Mercy cried.

You were in love? With who? The lawyer downstairs?

“I knew you were attracted to that lawyer downstairs, but you didn’t tell me you were dating him. And you *never* told me you were in love with him!” Grace said.

“The lawyer?” Mercy asked.

She thought about it for a second, and after the initial confusion left her, she realized she could confide in Grace after all, but she would never have to reveal *who* she'd made such a fatal mistake with. This was embarrassing enough without her sister lecturing her and scolding her about the culture differences between her and Seth. She had already become painfully aware that he would never marry her because she wasn't Amish. There would be no future for them because of it.

"Yes, that man broke my heart!" Mercy said, sobbing harder as her thoughts turned to Seth. "I just don't understand why he lied to me. He told me he loved me, but it was all to take advantage of me."

Mercy threw herself back into the soft depth of the pillows, letting fresh sobs rock her shoulders. Her head hurt, and her nose was so swollen she could barely breathe.

Grace's heart skipped a beat when she understood what Mercy had said to her. "You mean he…?"

She just couldn't say the words. They were even too awful to think about.

“He did not force me, if that’s what you’re asking.”

Grace’s eyes grew wide. “Well, then you…you had relations with him?”

“Yes, Grace!” she said angrily. “I did that. Go ahead and tell me what an awful person I am!”

Grace swallowed hard. Was she being judgmental of her sister? She wasn’t intending to be, but she had to admit, it was tough not to, given her upbringing. She knew that Mercy was counting on her to be supportive, and she would do her best to hide her real feelings about it.

“I am sorry that you’re going through this. I’m not going to tell you that you are an awful person. You thought you were in love, but that is why the Amish believe in marrying first—to avoid this kind of conflict between a man and a woman.”

“He asked me to marry him, but then he took it back—after,” Mercy sobbed. “I would not have let myself lose control like that if I hadn’t gotten so caught up in the romance of marrying him. Honest, I wouldn’t have. I was waiting for marriage, but now he’s taken that away from me, and I will never forgive him for it.”

"That is between him and *Gott,* Mercy. You should forgive him to clear your own conscience. I understand it might take some time, but you can't let this ruin your whole life. You are young, and you have your whole life ahead of you. In time, you will meet the right man, and you will be happy."

"It doesn't matter. I'm closing my heart to men for the rest of my life. If this is what they will do—lie to you to get their way with you, then I want nothing to do with them."

"They aren't all that way, Mercy. The Amish teach better morals than most of the world does. That is why we marry before having relations."

Mercy let out a guffaw. She wanted to tell Grace that it was an Amish man that had treated her this way, but it was pointless because she probably wouldn't believe her anyway.

"You are so naïve, Grace. Like I said, go back to your perfect world where you can turn a blind eye to the ways of the *Englisch.*"

Are you mocking the Amish?

"I want to stay here until you feel better," Grace protested.

Mercy jumped up from the sofa and went to the closet and pulled out a large suitcase. "Stay here, I don't care! But I'm leaving! I'm not going to stay here another minute!"

Grace suddenly felt awkward. "I'm sorry. You don't have to leave. I can go back and stay with *mei aenti."*

Mercy stopped for a second and looked at Grace. "You're not the one I'm mad at. I'm sorry if I'm taking it out on you. I don't mean to. But I have to go away for a while. I need to put some distance between me and…"

"*Him?"* Grace asked.

Mercy nodded. "Exactly! You can stay here while I'm gone, but I don't know when or if I'll be back!"

Grace felt a sudden emptiness in her gut. She didn't want to lose her sister over this, but she understood she was in pain and needed to get away.

"Where will you go?"

"My mother's parents live in New York, and I can go stay with them. Maybe I will stay and go to school there or find a real job so I don't have to depend on our dad so much."

Grace hugged her sister, holding her close.

"I will miss you," she sobbed.

"I didn't mean to make you cry," Mercy said, letting a fresh batch of tears go. "I will miss you too, but I'll write to you, I promise."

…It was a promise she would never keep.

CHAPTER35

Christmas Day, the following year…

Grace opened the front door and nearly tripped over a wicker basket on the porch. Had she left the laundry there after bringing it in from the barn? She'd been a little scatter-brained lately, but surely, she would never bring a basket of laundry to the front porch. She'd have brought it in through the kitchen.

I must have, she scolded herself. *Or it wouldn't be here.*

She glanced at the quilt stuffed into the basket that her *mamm* had made for her last birthday.

She'd needed a new one for some time, but after one of the barn cats had sneaked into the house and had her litter of kittens on it, Grace had not wanted the tattered quilt back. From that moment on, it had belonged to the cat, and so *mamm* had made her a new one.

I don't even remember washing that quilt, Grace chuckled to herself.

Leaving the basket for the time being, she grabbed the snow shovel that leaned against the side of the house and went toward the steps. Shoveling the short walkway was the last thing she had to do to get ready for her family's visit. Her Christmas pies had been baked, as had her cinnamon bread. Thanks to *Aenti* Sadie's teaching while she was in the city, her first family visit would be a success. Her *mamm* would be proud, and she would be able to impress Lilly without Mercy's help.

Ach, Mercy. I sure do miss you!

She pushed back thoughts of the past year, knowing that a lot of good had come from it too. She refused to let anything get her down today.

Grace looked up into the grey sky, watching wispy snowflakes flutter around in an endless swirl of white above her. Today was certainly going to be the most perfect birthday, and an even more perfect Christmas day.

Grace couldn't wait to see her family. It would be their first visit to her new home in the community. Though she'd not joined the church, she was grateful her family was still able to associate with her, as they did not belong to such a strict *Ordnung* that would not permit contact between them.

As she reached the bottom step of the porch, Grace swung back the shovel and dug into the snow that was several inches deep.

She paused before lifting the weight of it, thinking she'd heard something out of the ordinary. After a moment of listening to nothing but the dense, snowfall, she tossed the shovel-full to the side of the walkway with great effort. Jabbing the shovel under the next layer, she scraped across the concrete until she had a shovel-full.

The wind howled, but a familiar noise floated along the muffled, wintry air that circulated within a cocoon of snow-covered landscape. It always amazed her how the world was quieter beneath the snow-scattered sky and insulated layer of snow that covered the branches overhead. She'd always loved the Christmas season, but this year it seemed somehow bittersweet.

Grace had not been feeling like herself lately, no matter how much she tried to shake it. Perhaps it was the move back to the community that had her out-of sorts, but she had another suspicion—one she wasn't yet willing to admit even to herself.

Though she was happy to be back in the community, she'd had a tough year of disappointments with Mercy, whom she hadn't seen or heard from since the day she'd left her apartment when her *Englisch schweschder* had disappeared completely from her life. She'd left her apartment behind, which Grace had thought was strange since she'd just moved in, and she knew how much Mercy loved that apartment.

There had always been something strange about the last day she'd seen Mercy. That day still hadn't set right with Grace, but she'd not been able to figure it out. Even their father had complained that he'd lost contact with her, but sadly, that was not such a sacrifice for him.

Pushing her worries aside so she could make fast work of the short path she had left to shovel, Grace paused when she heard the noise again. She was distracted, that she was certain of, but was it enough to keep her from doing a chore that took not much more than five minutes?

There it is again, she said, pulling off her earmuffs so she could hear it better.

She paused again to listen.

It sounds like a baby crying!

Grace jabbed the shovel into the pile of snow she'd accumulated to the side of the walk, leaving it there as she followed the sound that made her heart skip a beat. She made her way up the porch steps cautiously, terrified of what she might actually find in the laundry basket where the noise seemed to be coming from.

The basket; that upon closer examination, wasn't even hers!

In fact, that quilt was a little different from hers. Oh, it was close, but it wasn't hers. She would know her *mamm's* stitching anywhere, and that was not it!

Grace leaned her head over the kitchen sink once more, allowing the last of her morning meal to escape her with a struggle. Was it just nerves, or was this more of what she'd first thought was the flu? She'd begun to fear she had found herself in the family way, and if so, she was in for more anxiety than what was brought on by the surprise that was left on her front porch!

Crossing the room with wobbly legs to the table where she'd left the wicker basket, she peered inside and looked at the wee one who wouldn't stop crying.

This is not happening to me!

Grace sucked in a deep breath, hoping she would not have to run to the sink for a second time this morning. Reaching into the basket, she lifted the baby from its cocoon of blankets and held it close to her. She stared with disbelief at the red and white stocking cap the infant was wearing, and the red snowsuit—an *Englisch* snowsuit. It was an expensive little suit, and she knew this from the time she'd spent in the city. She'd done a lot of window shopping and wishing for *Englisch* things, but in the end, had chosen to return to the community.

Her home had laid vacant for so many years, that from the outside, the place still looked abandoned. She'd only been living there for a little over a month, and being winter, outside repairs would have to wait until spring.

Who would know that anyone lived in this haus, as rundown as it looks from the outside?

Panic overtook her, but she managed to stay calm to keep the now-quiet infant in her arms calm. She pressed her face to the baby's forehead and breathed in. Grace loved the smell of newborn babies. There was just something soothing about the smell of a newborn's head. There was nothing else like it in the whole world. And although Grace was anxious to have her own family, she just wasn't certain she was ready for that just yet.

So what am I to do with this wee one, then?

Grace held the baby close, knowing that even though she was not the natural mother, the sound of her heartbeat would keep the infant calm. But how could she do that when her own heart rate would not slow down?

This is not happening, she repeated to herself.

She wandered over to the back door, but as she passed by the window, she could see through the window that there was no one there.

Who would have left you with me? I'm not ready to take care of a baby. I don't even know how I'm going to feed you!

Stay calm, she reassured herself. *I'm gut with the wee ones. After all, I spent a lot of time taking care of Jonah, and he was much smaller than you.*

She went to the sink for a glass of water hoping it would abate the nervous roiling of her stomach.

The wind howled and made her shiver as she peered out the window above the sink, watching icy snow pelting the glass.

It was Christmas day, and her family would be around soon enough to wish her a Happy Birthday, but she'd not heard the clip-clop of horse's hooves or the grinding of buggy wheels against the icy gravel in her driveway just yet.

She needed to think.

Panic suddenly coursed through her at the thought of gathering with her family for her twenty-second birthday and for First Christmas. Not only did she have an unknown baby in her arms, but if she, herself, was with child, she wasn't ready for anyone to know about it this soon.

Grossmammi Ellie was sure to figure it out. Being the community midwife for so long, she would surely pull her aside and call her out for it. Grace could no more process the reality of it herself; how would she be able to handle her entire family finding out all at once?

This was all just too overwhelming.

She wasn't yet ready to face the truth about it, so how could she possibly face so many family members all at once, asking questions, forcing their opinions on her, and trying to get her to commit to the community, and she wasn't ready for that either. With a baby on the way, she would be pressured to join the community and set things right in her life.

Grace sucked in a deep breath, as she made a mental note of how familiar the little red and white stocking hat was.

It's almost the same as the one mei mamm put on me before she left me on Grossmammi's doorstep!

A little cry startled her out of her thoughts.

There was only one thing that comforted her now; her *grossmammi* and *mamm* would certainly understand the predicament she was in with the special Christmas gift that was left on her front porch.

CHAPTER 36

Grace lightly rocked the baby in her arms, not knowing what else to do. She was suddenly eager to have her *mamm* arrive, but not just because she'd be bringing her favorite cake for her birthday; no, she was eager for her *mamm's* help. She never thought she would look forward to getting advice from her *mamm,* but she knew she was in way over her head with this.

The clip-clop of horse's hooves suddenly became music to her ears. She rushed to the front window, happy to see her family driving up the driveway toward her house. She blew out a sigh of relief—a breath she'd been holding in for too long.

Tempted to run out the door to greet them, she waited anxiously for them to come inside, knowing she had to stay with the baby.

She hoped the infant would be enough of a diversion to keep questions at bay regarding her own condition, but if she knew her family, they would bring it all out in the open for discussion.

Jonah ran up the porch ahead of the rest of the crowd and burst through Grace's front door. Surprise filled his eyes as he focused on the infant in his sister's arms.

"You had a baby while you were gone?"

Grace let a nervous giggle escape her lips.

"*Nee,* I'm watching the wee one for someone else," she stuttered.

It wasn't exactly a lie, but she couldn't tell her little brother that she'd found the baby on her doorstep. He was too young to understand such things and did not need to be involved with adult problems.

"Is it a boy or a girl?" he asked as he ran into the kitchen to set down the dish of food his *mamm* had entrusted him with.

"*Ach,*" Grace said with a shaky voice, realizing she had no idea if the infant was a boy or a girl. "You'll have to guess."

Jonah set the pie down on the table and suddenly seemed distracted by the basket.

"What's Mercy's quilt doing here? Did she come to see me?"

Grace could feel the sudden squeeze of her heart behind her ribcage as if she'd been trampled by a horse. "What makes you think that's Mercy's quilt?"

"Because I helped her put the squares together," he said lifting a corner of the fabric. "She made certain I followed the same rows as the quilt *mamm* made for you."

Tears pooled in Grace's eyes as she dipped her head down to the kiss the child that could possibly be her niece or nephew. If the baby belonged to Mercy, how was she ever going to explain this to her *mamm,* especially when it made no sense even to her? More than that, she would have to explain to her that Mercy had taken her place and pretended to be her while she continued to stay in the city.

Fresh anxiety coursed through her veins as she heard the rest of her family enter from the front door. Her *mamm* called out to her, but Grace shook with fear and could not seem to find her voice.

"She's in here with the baby," Jonah called, ratting her out.

Grace knew he probably didn't realize what he'd done, and it wasn't like she was going to be able to hide it from her family, but she was about to have to face them, ready or not.

CHAPTER 37

Grace looked at her *mamm* sheepishly as she entered the kitchen wearing a welcoming smile. Her expression turned pale when she caught sight of the infant wearing the red and white striped stocking hat in her daughter's arms.

"What is the meaning of this, Grace?" she asked curtly. "Whose baby is that?"

She almost sounded angry with Grace.

Her Grandma Ellie entered the room just then and ushered the rest of the family out of the room—mainly Jonah, who protested until she quietly reprimanded him.

"I'm waiting for an answer," her *mamm* said impatiently. "And why have you put that cap on her head?"

"I didn't, *mamm,"* Grace defended. "I'm not sure if the baby is a boy or a girl, but I promise you, it came this way—with the hat on! But it's not the same one. *Mine* is still at your *haus* back in my old bedroom."

Her *mamm* shook her head. "It looks the same to me! And what do you mean the baby *came that way?"*

Grace swallowed down the lump of fear that clogged her throat. "Someone left the baby on my front porch just a short time ago!"

Her *mamm* staggered backward into a chair.

Had history repeated itself?

No one in the community had known what she'd done twenty-two years ago, had they? She looked at her daughter, who lightly rocked the baby in her arms. It was like looking at herself in the mirror.

Anna couldn't catch her breath. Who would have known what had happened all those years ago—

enough to repeat the same act in the same way? She stared at her daughter and the baby—the *Englisch* baby!

Or was it?

She, herself, had gone to great lengths to make Ellie believe the baby she'd left at her doorstep was also *Englisch.* So why was this baby's mother mimicking what she'd done, and why was the infant left on her daughter's porch? Was someone playing a cruel trick on them?

"Who did you tell about this?" her *mamm* accused her, as she stood and touched the little cap on the baby's head.

"I haven't told anyone—except..."

It suddenly registered that she had told Mercy the story of what her *mamm* had done, but it had been in the utmost confidence. She'd not done it to bring shame on her *mamm's* head. They'd merely swapped stories of how they'd come to be the daughters of the same man.

"Who?" her *mamm* pressed.

"I'm sorry, *mamm.* I didn't tell her to hurt you. I told Mercy."

"Mercy?"

"*Mei schweschder.*"

Anna collapsed into the chair at the table in her daughter's kitchen. She was as pale as the linen table cloth.

Grandma Ellie entered the room and lifted the baby from Grace's arms.

She pulled one of the blankets from the basket and set the baby down on the table. She made fast work of undressing the baby, making a thorough examination as she did.

"The umbilical cord is almost healed, which means this child is most likely about three weeks old. I can see a compression on the end of the cord from a clamp, showing that the birth took place in a hospital. The paper diaper could be from the hospital too—it looks generic."

Pulling off the diaper to change the baby, Grandma Ellie had finished her assessment. "It's a girl!" she said as she replaced the diaper with one that was in the basket. "Funny, but this is almost the same way I found *you,*" she said to Grace.

Grace turned to her *mamm.* “I’m sorry for telling her about something that was so private, but I was angry at the time, and I didn’t understand what you were going through then. And I’m sorry that this is upsetting you so much.”

Anna stood and pulled her daughter into her arms. “I need you to forgive me for what I did.”

“I have already forgiven you,” Grace promised. “I know you were only doing what you thought was best for me, and I know you were a scared, young girl. I’m happy the way things turned out. I’m blessed that you are *mei mamm,* and I’m blessed to have a *daed* that loves me as much as his own *kinner.”*

She looked at the baby in her grandma’s arms.

“Mercy isn’t as lucky as I am, and if that is her *dochder,* I need to help her!”

CHAPTER 38

Simon Bontrager finished the last of his daily chores, making certain the animals were settled down in the warmth of the barn before he made his way to the house. As he opened the barn door, he could smell his Christmas dinner, and it made his mouth water. More than that, his heart warmed despite the snow and wind that assaulted him because he knew how hard his new bride had worked to make it perfect for him.

Several buggies filled his long driveway, and he was happy that the family had made it through the deep snow so they could gather for First Christmas instead of tomorrow like was normal. It was a special day for his *fraa,* and he couldn't wait for the special gift she'd promised him. He'd made her something special, hoping she'd have some news for him that would make his gift appropriate.

He pulled open the kitchen door and stomped his boots on the top step before entering. Before he had a chance to take off his heavy wool coat, his gaze met up with his *fraa.* She looked as pale as the snow, and her cheeks were pink.

He rushed to her side, walking past the family members gathered in the small kitchen.

"Are you sick again, Grace?"

She nodded. "A little, but that isn't what's wrong."

His expression dropped. "What's wrong?"

She pointed to the infant in her grandmother's arms. "I found her on the front porch when I went out to shovel."

Tears welled up in her eyes. "I don't know what would have happened if I hadn't gone out there when I did."

"Do you know who the *boppli* belongs to? Was there a note in the basket like there was with you?"

Grace hadn't even thought to look for a note. She'd been so worried about what she was going to do with the baby that she hadn't thought past that. She went to the basket and began to dig through it until she found a note with her name on the front of the envelope.

Her breath caught in her throat. She didn't have to read the letter to know it was from Mercy, but why?

Tears filled her eyes, and Simon pulled her into his arms, ushering everyone else out of the kitchen to give Grace some room to breathe. Even he knew she needed some time to recover from the shock. He'd heard all about Mercy but had never had the chance to meet her since she'd gone off to New York just before he and Grace had begun seriously dating. She hadn't even attended the wedding they'd had in the city despite Grace's multiple attempts at contacting Mercy through their father. Sadly, he didn't know how to contact his daughter any more than Grace did.

When she calmed down, Grace sat in a chair and put a hand on the quilt her sister had made. It was beautiful, she had to admit. She was not able to make such a beautiful piece, and she deeply admired her sister's work. Fingering the letter, Grace knew she could not put off reading the contents even a moment longer. She lifted the flap to the envelope and pulled out a one-page note, a legal document, and a birth certificate.

She looked at the name on it. *Elizabeth Grace Pritchard.*

She'd named her baby after Grace!

In the area where it stated the mother, she read the name, *Mercy Grace Pritchard.*

All this time, she never knew they had a name in common, and she had to wonder if it was a mere coincidence or if it had been intentional on their father's part.

Grace's heart did a somersault when she read the legal document naming her and Simon as the legal guardians of little Elizabeth.

Something was not right about the document. She couldn't put her finger on it just yet, but she hoped she would figure it out once she had calmed down. Until then, she would have to accept it for what it was.

She paused before reading the short note.

Was she ready to hear what Mercy had to say?

Dear Grace,

I know this comes as a shock to you, but I had nine long months to make this decision. It was not an easy one, but one that I knew must take place. I've had a difficult time caring for her on my own for the two weeks that I waited for the legal papers to be drawn up. She is now nearly three weeks old, and bottle-fed. I've enclosed all the things you need to get started. I didn't expect that you would have any bottles in your new home.

Congratulations, by the way on your marriage. I'm sorry I couldn't be there.

Please understand that the day you last saw me I was too emotional to make a wise decision about Elizabeth since I'd just taken a pregnancy test about an hour before you'd arrived at my apartment. I assure you that the last nine months has been spent carefully weighing my options, and I concluded every time that my child would be better off in a home with two parents who loved and cared for her.

Being raised by a father who wasn't your biological parent, makes you the best person to understand the situation, and I am confident she will find love and happiness in your home with you as a mother, and that you will love her as if she was your own child.

Don't try to find me because I will not change my mind, and this decision was painful enough without anyone putting pressure on me to undo what is already done.

Tell her that I loved her enough to make this decision for her.

Thank you for respecting my wishes.

Your Sister,

Mercy

Grace slammed the letter down on the table.

"I have to find her!"

Simon tried to comfort her, but she would not be consoled.

Grace lowered Elizabeth into the cradle that her husband had so lovingly made for their own child. She would not soon forget the look on his face when she'd shared the news she suspected. She settled herself into the bed beside him and he rolled over sleepily and laid a hand on her belly. Soon enough they would have a child of their own to care for.

Turning her head toward the cradle beside the bed, Grace wondered how she would handle two infants so close together in age if she could not convince Mercy to raise her own child. It wasn't that she did not want to raise Elizabeth, but she knew Mercy had so much love to give the child, and she would gladly help her in any way she could to reunite with Elizabeth.

She didn't expect Mercy to be at her apartment, so she would start with the lawyer tomorrow. Since Mercy had let it be known that he was the one she'd fallen in love with, perhaps he could help convince her not to give up her child.

But would he marry her and help her raise Elizabeth?

CHAPTER 39

Simon pulled his buggy up to the curb in front of Mercy's building. He turned to his wife and admired the look of her holding the infant, and knowing she would soon hold his child, warmed his heart.

"Are you sure this is the right thing to do?" he asked.

"I'm not certain if it will make things worse, and I pray it won't, but I would never be able to live with myself if I didn't at least try to help *mei schweschder.*"

Before she could get up the curb, the lawyer was walking up to the building. She'd only spoken to him a handful of times during her stay in Mercy's apartment all those months she was in the city dating Simon. She'd always been respectful, but curt with him after hearing the way he'd treated her sister. She'd always wanted to tell him what she thought of him, and now she was so angry, she wasn't certain she would be able to act with kindness and forgiveness as was the Amish way.

The man put his key in the door and entered his office, the pretty brunette on his arm planting a kiss full on his mouth before she walked back to her car that was parked in front of their buggy.

Grace fumed at his obvious lack of propriety.

Pulling Elizabeth close to her, she followed behind him and into his office. She stood at the door for a moment and stared blankly at the name on the glass.

Then it dawned on her.

She pulled the letter out from her pocket with her free hand and looked at the legal document. The man had prepared the document himself! He was just as Mercy had claimed. He was a *pig* and didn't care about her or his child.

Grace paused and looked back at her husband, who sat respectfully in the buggy and waited for her the way she'd asked him to. Then she placed a kiss on the baby's head. Was Elizabeth better off with them than with a man who cared so little that he would sign away his child so carelessly, and for no other reason than he obviously loved himself and that other woman more than Mercy or Elizabeth. It pained her to think such a thing could be true, but she would try her best to give him the benefit of the doubt ringing in her mind.

By the time she reached his waiting room, Grace was unable to control her emotions.

He greeted her at his office door. "I've been expecting you, Grace. Come into my office so we can talk."

Grace held up the letter in her fist and shook it at him. "I'm not certain there is much to say. I think Mercy's letter and this legal paper says it all. What is the meaning of this?"

"I know you are only seeing the negative side to this, but I need you to see the positive side too. This is not such a bad thing for her since she was unable to care for the baby herself."

Grace pursed her lips and glared at him.

"She wouldn't have to take care the baby on her own if you would have stepped up and helped her!"

He cleared his throat. "Don't think I didn't try. I offered to marry her about a month before she had the baby, but she turned me down!"

"Well, perhaps that was to give you a taste of your own medicine!" Grace accused.

"For what?" he asked, confusion clouding his expression. "For trying to help her when it wasn't my responsibility?"

"How can you sit there and say that this child is not your responsibility? Have you no conscience?"

"Elizabeth is not my child," he said.

CHAPTER 40

"What do you mean she isn't your child?" Grace practically shrieked. "Are you accusing *mei schweschder* of being a loose woman?"

Grace knew it was one of those questions that appeared it should be answered positively, but in reality, it was not.

"Of course not!" he shot back. "Mercy and I are friends, nothing more."

"Then why would you offer to marry her if you are not the father of her child?"

"Mercy and I were never anything more than friends, and we were never *intimate,"* he said quietly.

Grace bounced the baby in her arms, trying not to share her anxiety with Elizabeth.

“If you’re not the father, then did she tell you who is?”

He shook his head. “I asked her and she wouldn’t give me a name, but she did say he was Amish.”

“What? Who?”

He shrugged.

Grace tried hard to remember conversations she’d had with her sister nearly a year ago, and she could no more think of who it could be than she could imagine Mercy’s involvement with someone from her own community.

One thing was certain. There were only two men in the community who were single, and one of them was an older widower, so that left one—Henry Yoder. She would ask Henry, who was only nineteen at the time, but she felt it useless and unlikely Mercy would fall in love with him. It just didn’t make sense to Grace, but then, nothing about this made sense to her.

Grace readied herself to make a visit to the Yoder farm to speak with Henry. Simon would not be able to go with her, but made her promise not to go alone, and so she was waiting on Jonah to help her. This was not going to be an easy visit for her since she barely knew him, and normally this was something that her husband should handle, but since they hadn't joined the community, Simon left it to her discretion to break protocol.

Jonah entered the kitchen just as she was bundling Elizabeth in the little red snowsuit Mercy had put her in. "Why are we making a visit to the Yoder's?"

It was a reasonable question, but Grace didn't know quite how to answer her little brother without exposing Mercy's indiscretion.

"Are we going over there to see if he's Elizabeth's *daed?"*

"Ach, where did you hear that?"

"I'm thirteen years old, Grace! Do you think I don't hear things?"

Grace pursed her lips and shook her head at him. "I suppose you do, but we will not gossip. We must protect Mercy's reputation."

"I understand," he said. "But why don't you ask Seth if he knows?"

Grace felt her heart tighten and her breath heaved. "Why should we ask Seth?"

"Because Mercy was *gut* friends with him while she was here."

"What do you mean, Jonah?" she asked slowly.

"He came to pick her up every day when she was here. He even took her for a sleigh ride, and I saw her kiss him once."

"Jonah, please tell me you are not making up stories?"

"I'm not! I'm too old for that. I promise," he said, his brow furrowed.

"I believe you," she said. "But if that is true then you're right. We need to go see Seth first."

Grace packed up Elizabeth in the back of the buggy, and the three of them were on their way to finding out the truth.

At least Grace prayed it was so.

CHAPTER 41

Grace pulled into the yard in front of the barn at the Yoder farm—the other Yoder farm, which was Henry's cousin, Seth. She was not certain she was mentally prepared for the talk she was about to have with him, especially since the last talk she'd had with him had not gone smoothly.

As she reflected on that day, sudden panic coursed through her as she realized his confusion about their breakup that day. Had she made him so upset that he broke up with Mercy? Was this all her fault?

Pushing aside her fears, she gathered Elizabeth in her arms and headed toward the barn where she knew she could find Seth. He and his *daed* were the harness makers of the community, and they worked out of their barn.

She opened the door cautiously and called out to him, warning him of her presence.

He came from the back of the barn where there work room was, but she stayed near the door to keep out of the wind with the baby.

He tipped his hat cordially. "You are the last person I would expect to see. Didn't you just get married?"

She nodded. "*Jah,* I did.'

"Then shouldn't you be at home with your husband?"

He was still angry.

"He knows I'm here," she answered curtly.

He shifted his feet and sighed as he removed his hat and ran his hand through his thick hair.

"Then what are you doing here? I thought we said our peace already. If you need harnesses you can have your husband do business with *mei daed.*"

He started to walk away.

“Wait Seth,” she said. “We need to talk.”

He looked at the baby and then at her, his expression turning pale. “What could you and I possibly have to talk about, Grace?”

She turned the baby around for him to see.

“I have reason to believe Elizabeth belongs to you.”

His eyes widened. “You have reason to believe she’s mine? Don’t you know for sure?”

Off went his hat and the hand went through the hair like a mad man. It was what he did when he couldn’t deal with stress, and Grace knew it. She now knew she would have to use her words carefully in order to fix this and keep Mercy’s dignity intact.

“*Nee,* I don’t know for certain if she’s yours, but I suspect she is.”

“What does your *husband* have to say about all of this, Grace?’ he asked angrily.

“We both want to find out the truth.”

He swiped his hat off his head again and ran a vigorous hand through his hair. "Well just how many other men were there*?"*

Grace leered at him. "Just what are you implying, Seth Yoder?"

"That if you don't know who fathered your own child, then you *must* have been with more men than me!"

"This child is not mine!" Grace practically shrieked.

"Then what makes you think I'm the father?"

"What makes you think you and I were together that way, Seth?"

"I didn't imagine it no matter how much you might want to deny it."

"When was it that you believe you and I were together that way?" she asked cautiously.

He looked at Elizabeth nervously. "I'd have to confess it had to have been right around the same time that this wee one had to have been conceived."

She knew then it was Mercy he'd been with.

"Then it's true," she said. "You must be Elizabeth's father."

"How do you figure that to be true if you're not her *mamm?*" he asked, confusion taking over his expression.

She paused, trying to choose her words carefully, but no matter how many times she ran it over in her mind, it came out the same way in the end.

"Because you were with *mei schweschder,* Mercy, not me!"

"Now wait a minute Sweet Pea," he said, it suddenly dawning on him. "You are not my Sweet Pea, are you?"

Grace shook her head thoughtfully. "I'm afraid I'm not."

"But you broke up with me."

"I did that as a formality to free me for pursuing Simon. Do you forget that we were engaged?"

"Oh no!" he said. "When you broke up with me I thought it was her—you—my Sweet Pea, that was breaking up with me. I said hurtful things…did you come back after you broke up with me to talk to me again?"

Grace shook her head. "I didn't. It must have been Mercy."

"I'm a little confused. Her name is Mercy? I didn't know you had a twin. Where has she been all this time?"

"We are not twins. We have the same *daed*, but not the same *mamm*. *Mei mamm* had a *relationship* before she married *mei daed*—the one that raised me—Jacob. This man had a relationship close after with Mercy's *mamm,* but she wasn't Amish. We swapped places last year so I could stay in the city for a while because I was angry after hearing all this news about *mei familye,* and I met Mercy there. She decided she wanted to see how the Amish lived and when I returned she told me what a happy time she had here. Now I know why."

Seth pulled his hat off again and nearly rubbed his head bald. "I must have hurt her badly with the way I talked to her that day. But I was so hurt when you—I thought you were the one who broke up with me, but I guess it was her the whole time."

Grace nodded. "*Jah,* she was very hurt. She was in love with you, Seth, and I think it messed everything up."

Grace began to cry.

"I'm so sorry I did this, but I had no idea what was going on with the two of you. If I had I would have never messed with your business."

"I love her too, Grace, and I would never hurt her. I need to find her and make her forgive me."

He held his arms out to Elizabeth, tears welling up in his eyes. "She's really mine?"

"It looks that way," she said. "Mercy signed her over to me and Simon, but we can figure out what to do about that later."

Seth nodded, holding his daughter close.

CHAPTER 42

Seth looked at Grace's directions closer, making certain he had found the correct building. She had wanted to go with him to help explain the mistake that he'd made in thinking it was Mercy that had broken up with him, but Seth assured Grace it was something he needed to do alone.

He took a deep breath, walked into the building and up the stairs to her apartment, pausing before knocking on the door.

She opened the door and stared at him with sad eyes. "What are you doing here?" she muttered quietly.

He knelt down on one knee and looked up at her whimsically. "I believe this is how the *Englischers* do this, *jah?"*

The corners of her mouth turned up with light amusement.

"I suppose it depends on what you're trying to do."

"I am trying to propose to you Sweet Pea—again, but this time to you as *Mercy."*

Tears welled up in her eyes, and she pushed down the reality that he must have thought she was Grace when he originally proposed. And thought it hurt her, she realized it was her he loved and not her sister.

"I want to make a *familye* with you and Elizabeth. She's beautiful."

"Well, she should be," Mercy said. "She looks just like her daddy—her *daed."*

Seth stood up and pulled her into his arms.

"I'm so sorry I hurt you, but Grace came to *mei haus* and broke off our engagement, and I thought it was you. But you have to understand, I fell in love with *you* not Grace. We were only engaged before out of obligation, but when I took you for that sleigh ride, I thought something had changed in her as if she was a whole different person. It turns out she was, and I'm happy it was you I fell in love with. I didn't mean to break your heart, and I'm sorry I wasn't with you and our *dochder* this whole time."

Mercy shook with sobs in his arms. Part from relief and part mourning over the loss of time with the man she loved.

"But I made a legal document naming Grace and Simon as her parents."

"Don't worry. Grace said she would burn that piece of paper if you'll come back and have me as your husband so we can be a *familye."*

"You broke up with me! And you thought I was my sister!"

"I didn't know it was you, or I would never have let you go. I love you, Mercy."

"Say it again," she said.

"Say what?" he asked.

"Call me by the right name so I know that you know who I am!" she said with a smile.

"I love you, Mercy! Will you marry me, then?"

"*Jah,*" she said. "I will marry you, but don't ever break up with me again!"

"You will never have to worry about that again," he promised her.

He planted his lips firmly on hers, and she deepened the kiss that she thought she would never feel from his lips again. She had not stopped loving him, but she hadn't been able to imagine her life without him, and now she wouldn't have to.

It didn't matter to him that she was not Amish. He loved her unconditionally, and she loved him the same. Joy filled her heart as the reality sunk in that she would be able to raise her daughter that she missed and loved so much with the man that she also missed and loved.

Boy, am I going to need Grace's help!

CHAPTER 43

Grace pulled the bread out of the oven, while Mercy set the table for dinner. Elizabeth gurgled at Seth when he tickled her tummy and she couldn't help but smile at the blessing that was her *familye.*

Mercy patted Grace's stomach. "It won't be long now before you have that wee one, and Elizabeth will have a little cousin to play with."

She hugged her sister, feeling overwhelmed by the blessings they shared. With Mercy and Seth married and living in their *dawdi haus,* she could not be happier.

Lilly came into the kitchen just then and smiled at the two of them as she picked up Elizabeth. "I still can't believe I'm going to be an *aenti.* Can you hurry up and have that *boppli, Grace?"*

"Ach, Lilly, you're already an *aenti.* Look how Elizabeth takes to you."

She lightly bounced Elizabeth in her arms.

"I'm trying to get in lots of practice so that when your wee one arrives, I will be an experienced *aenti,"* she beamed.

Lilly bounded out of the room to let her sister do the cooking for a change. She was no longer interested in being a show-off in the kitchen, she had something more important to occupy her time.

Mercy turned to Grace and smiled with a far-off look in her eyes.

"What's the matter, dear, *schweschder?"* Grace asked.

"I'm grateful for all the help you've given me and shown me how to be a good mother to Elizabeth. I still can't believe I thought that bringing her here and leaving her on your doorstep was the only solution I had."

Grace smiled. "I'm certain you will be bringing her back the first time she talks back to you!"

"I'm sure you're right," Mercy said.

They both laughed heartily as they finished preparing the meal for the *familye* that Mercy now shared with Grace.

THE END

Stay connected with me:

PLEASE SIGN up for my mailing list HERE!

www.SamanthaBayarr.com

Email me at SamanthaBayarr@gmail.com

Her
Amish
Heart
Samantha Bayarr

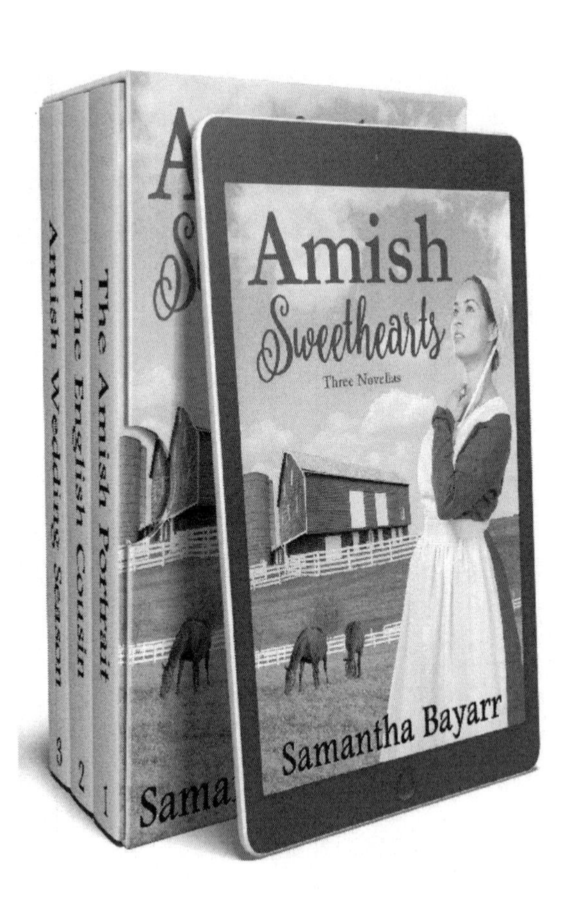
The Amish Portrait 1
The English Cousin 2
Amish Wedding Season 3
Amish
Sweethearts
Three Novellas
Samantha Bayarr

Made in the USA
Middletown, DE
12 May 2023